my new
forever

CARA WADE

First published May 2021

Copyright © Cara Wade 2021

Published by Crooked Crown Publishing

Cover design by Cara Wade

Developmental and copy editing provided by Kendra Gaither at Kendra's Editing and Book Services

To the boys in my life. Thank you.

PROLOGUE
MASON

S he's gone.

My Ella. Gone.

I knew things were bad when hospice was called in to "make her comfortable." The woman was fucking dying. How do you make someone comfortable? She was only thirty-four, for Christ's sake! How the fuck am I supposed to care for Amber and Teddy without her? My kids are only three and two. They aren't even going to remember her.

She's going to be a forgotten memory, especially for Teddy. He's too young to understand what's going on. I don't even know if anyone has told him yet.

I sure as hell haven't.

Ella was the rock that held us all together. I don't know how to relate to my kids, but *she* did. She always knew the right things to say and what they needed. She knew how to kiss scrapes and gave the best hugs.

It should have been me.

I had refused to let her stay in that fucking hospital bed in the living room. *No.* She was my wife and belonged in *our* bed. With me.

The night before she died, the four of us spent time together, cuddling and talking. Ella had been too weak to do anything but lie in bed, so we made a night out of it. Amber was telling us all about some game she invented. I have no idea what the rules were, as they seemed to change and contradict themselves, but Ella was all smiles listening to her little girl.

Teddy was curled up in her lap, his head resting on her shoulder as he played with her thinning hair. It's as if he could sense something wasn't right and didn't want to let go. He's always been a kind and cuddly little boy, so it shouldn't have been surprising.

Finally, it was late and both kids had fallen asleep. I moved them into their own rooms, tucked them in, and hurried back to bed, knowing I was going to lose her any day now. *I can't fucking lose her.*

"Mason. Will you make love to me?" she asked as I closed the door to our room, cocooning us in our own little world.

My eyebrows drew tight and I shook my head. I didn't want to add any more stress to her body. "We shouldn't, baby," I said, sitting on the side of the bed, stroking her tear-stained cheek.

"Please, Mason. I need you. I need you to make me feel whole again, even if it's just for the night." She wrapped her hand around mine and kissed my knuckles. "I don't know how much time I have left, and I know it's selfish to ask this of you, but I want to feel like your special girl, just one more time." She sniffled and closed her eyes, warding off my looks of pity. "Don't," she said firmly. Her throat bobbed as she held back her tears.

"Don't what?" I asked her, keeping my voice as even as I could.

"I don't want your pity, Mason. I want your *love*. I want to know that when I'm gone, you're going to take good care of our kids. They're half of me, you know. I'll never truly be gone as long as you love them."

I swallowed thickly. I'm a big man, I don't cry, but her words brought me to my knees. "I know, baby."

"Then make love to me tonight. Show me how much I mean to you, and I promise this is the last time I will ask for it." My stomach dropped and I felt sick. *She won't ask for it again because she knows she will be gone.* She placed her hand on my cheek and gave me a sad smile before a coughing fit took over.

I jumped up, grabbing a towel and helping her sit up in bed to ease some of her discomfort. After a minute, her coughing stopped and her mucus-filled breaths seemed to echo in the still air.

"You won't break me," she pleaded.

I kissed her temple, cradling her head in the crook of my neck, and the two of us rocked back and forth as her tears stained my t-shirt until she finally fell asleep from exhaustion. I held her long enough to memorize her soft features. Even though the sickness had changed the way she looked on the outside, she would always be my beautiful girl.

I didn't sleep that night. I couldn't. I knew it was coming, I could hear it in her breathing. Each breath was more labored than the last. I took her hand in mine and held it until I could no longer hear her breathing and felt her skin grow cold under my fingertips.

Tears dropped down my cheeks in rivers as I muffled my cries in her shoulder.

Gone.

Amber crawled into our bed the next morning after the hearse had come to collect Ella's body, curling her tiny frame against my back side.

"Where's Mommy, Daddy?" Her sad voice broke me from my dark thoughts.

I didn't even have the courage to look at my little girl, who looked so much like her mother. "Gone. She's not coming back." My voice held no emotion. Ella's words haunted me about taking care of our kids, and I dragged her over my body and pulled her against my chest, rubbing the back of her head.

Her bright eyes looked up to my face, searching for answers. "Why?"

"Because she was sick and went to a better place."

I couldn't be having this conversation with her. I heard Teddy in his crib, babbling to himself, and I knew they needed breakfast, and both probably needed diaper changes, but I couldn't handle that right now. I texted Sharon, our next-door neighbor, and asked if she could take the kids for a while. She responded back seconds later, telling me she would be right over.

I went through the motions at her wake and funeral—accepting the looks and words of sympathy. Acting thankful for their kind thoughts and prayers, all the while wishing I could punch a hole through the wall with my fist and scream at the top of my lungs. My brothers, Maxwell and Matthew, and sister, Mallory, had come in from out of town to be here for me, and I'm thankful as fuck for that. They watched the kids as I drowned my sorrows in the bottom of a bottle.

Even some of my other friends from Falls Village, my hometown, made the trip to Portland to be here for me. It was nice to see them, but I wished it was for a happier celebration.

As the priest said a few more words that were somehow

supposed to make this whole thing easier, I tossed my red rose into her grave and turned away. The tie around my neck was like a noose, so I pulled at the dark fabric, trying to get some air into my lungs.

———————

I take another swig from the bottle of amber liquid on my nightstand. My eyes gloss over again as I stare at the wall. I've been lying in this bed for the past five days, with the exception of the funeral. There's been no reason to get up.

Amber and Teddy, the small voice, *her voice,* says in my mind.

"Mason, I know you're hurting, but you need to get out of your drunken stupor and get your ass back in gear. You can't stay like this. Your family needs you," Mallory, my baby sister chastises from the doorway.

"Leave me alone," I grouse, not even bothering to look at her.

Amber pushes her way into my room and crawls onto the bed. "Daddy, pweese," she says, her soft voice pleading.

"Get out of here, Amber. Go play with Teddy."

"No, Daddy. Pweese get up," she cries as she takes my hand, tugging it in her little one.

"Go away, Amber!" I yell at her as I turn to stare her down, my teeth bared to her and my face flushed in anger.

Her entire body flinches and her chin quivers in fear. She gets off the bed quickly and runs away, her cries following her out the door. *Fuck.* I've never yelled at my kids like this.

"Amber, wait," I try, but I know she's already gone to hide in the fort in her room she calls her castle.

Mallory's look is one that could kill. She storms over to me, pulls the bottle of whiskey out of my hand, and slams it down on the table next to me. "What the fuck was that, Mason?" I shake my head, at a loss for words. "I know your wife just died, and I am so sorry for that. I can't even imagine what it would be like to lose Kevin forever, but you need to get your head out of your ass." She points down the hallway. "You have two little kids who need their father right now, and you're acting like a complete asshole.

"I'm taking them back to Falls Village with me. Clearly, they won't be taken care of if left here, and I refuse to let you ruin their lives. The renovation of Falls Village is happening and we need you. I need you, your brothers need you, and most importantly, your kids need you."

She turns and walks out of my room without a second glance.

CHAPTER ONE
MASON

The familiar coastline comes into view as some of the shops of Main Street elicit a small sense of emotion from me. I take a deep breath and push it through my nose. I spent too many years wandering up and down these streets as a boy, looking to keep my brothers out of trouble. If the James brothers were around, trouble wasn't far behind.

It didn't take me long after Mallory took my kids to get my head out of my ass and call a moving company to come and pack up my stuff. I have a realtor who is working on selling my house in Portland, but in the meantime, Mallory and Kevin are letting us stay with them until I can get us a place of our own.

It's only been a few weeks, but when I finally managed to get the courage to ask to speak with Amber, she hung up on me. *She definitely has her mom's temper.* Teddy, at least, will be happy to see me, but I know I've hurt Amber and she might take a while to warm up to me again.

I can fix this.

I pull into an empty spot along the beach and get out, breathing in the salty air. Mallory is expecting me soon, but I

need a little more time before I face her again. I know she's
happy to have the kids, but me... not so much.

I lock my door and walk to the bench close by, so I can
watch the people walking along the shore and the street.
People watching used to be something Ella and I did in
college. She loved guessing what someone's life was like just
from the few moments of seeing them stroll by. We used to get
a coffee and watch from afar.

The thought of her brings a smile to my face, which goes
away just as suddenly as the memory of her death takes its
place. I scrub my hand down my face, scratching my beard as I
look around me at the mostly familiar shoreline.

So much of this place has changed since I left. I couldn't
stay here. My dreams were too big for that. I graduated from
high school, was accepted at NYU, and didn't look back.
Growing up, my family didn't have a lot of money, until they
won the lottery and I knew I wanted a better life than that.
Fast money fucked shit up.

I worked construction to get me through my accounting
degree. Let me tell you, hard labor does a number for one's
body. I was always a fit guy, and I'm aware I turned a lot of
heads in high school, but that job made my body rock hard.
Which is why I was so surprised when I managed to catch the
attention of Ella Scranton.

She tried so hard to push me away. Each time she pushed,
I pulled her right back. From the moment I met her, my entire
world revolved around her. She was the light in my darkness.
Before I was even finished with my degree, I was saving for a
ring. She deserved nothing but the best, and I was going to give
it to her.

She definitely had the best years of my life, no matter how
short they were. I knew she wasn't going to live a long life, but I

didn't care. She was mine. My Ella. She had cystic fibrosis, having been diagnosed with it when she was little. She lived a normal life, but because of it, was always hesitant to let people in.

Except for me and the kids.

I shake the memories away and try to wrap my head around how I'm going to handle raising my kids on my own. I gave Mallory the go-ahead to enroll Amber in preschool, and Teddy goes to daycare now during the days. I have a meeting with the director, Hannah Bailey, next week since she wanted to meet me personally.

"Hey, man. It's been a while, I didn't expect to see you in town yet," my friend Cody Alexander says, slapping me on the shoulder. He's started going by Cole, his middle name, but I've known him too long to toe the line and call him that. I offer him a smile as he sits down next to me, watching a few people walk along the shore. Cody and I were friends growing up and have stayed in touch over the years.

"Yeah, I decided I needed to get out of Portland and start sorting my life out again. I can't hide forever." I sigh. "Plus, Mallory roped me into the town renovation and my brothers are back, so it makes sense to be around family that can help."

"How's Ella's family doing?" He looks down at his clasped hands hanging between his legs.

"About as good as they can, I suppose." I rub my forehead. "I can't be around them right now. It's too much. Everything in my old life is too much right now. I'm taking a step back, going to help with building up the town. *Actually* build it. It's been a long time since I've done work like this, and I need it."

"It'll be good to have you back in town. Although, I'm not sure the town can handle all the James brothers back here," he teases.

"Fuck off, man," I say, smiling. "You were always just jealous that I could catch more tail than you could."

He laughs hard. "I got my fair share, you know."

I shake my head, and my smile fades again. "I should probably get going. Mallory isn't a very patient person, and I'm sure she's ready to start bossing me around as soon as I step foot in her house." My lips curl into a grimace at the thought of living with her and her husband.

My sister had a good thing with her ex-husband, Joey. Financially, he could take care of her, give her everything she wanted. Kevin... not so much. Although, I will say, she seems a lot happier with him than she ever did with Joey, so I guess that's something.

I stand and stretch, working a few kinks out of my neck. "I'll catch you later." I wave and walk across the street to a small coffee shop, *Spill the Tea*. The bell above the door rings as Colleen Hamilton, the owner, steps into view.

"Mason," she says, offering me a warm smile. She comes around the counter, her full hips knocking into a small table as she extends her arms out. I bend down, letting her give me a hug, and she pats my back. "I'm so sorry to hear about your wife," she says quietly before letting me go.

"Thanks." I clear my throat and swallow past the lump. "What happened to the taffy shop?" I ask, looking around.

"We still sell it, but I upgraded and made it into a coffee shop, too." She steps back to look at me, small wrinkles forming around her eyes. "Brings in more tourists. Can I get you something? On the house."

I run my fingers through my hair. "Thanks, just a coffee with cream." I look at the sugary treats behind the glass and think of the kids. "How about two of those vanilla cupcakes, too, for the kids."

She pulls the treats out and places them in a box, tying a string around them, then hands me a coffee. When I try to hand her a twenty-dollar bill, she waves her hands at it and refuses to accept it. I stuff it into the tip jar, much to her chagrin.

"Thanks, Colleen. See you around." I walk out the door and back to my car. Hopefully, the cupcakes will help with my problem of Amber not talking to me.

CHAPTER TWO
HANNAH

*A*mber James is definitely something else. Taylor Hamilton, one of the teachers, has been trying to get her to open up more in class, but she seems to be struggling to do so. There's also the small matter of hitting another girl in the class. When Taylor asked Amber why she hit her, she said she didn't know. I think some of that has to do with her home life. I've had conversations with her Aunt Mallory, but I really need to speak with her father, Mason.

I hope he doesn't miss this meeting.

I glance down at my watch and see he has five more minutes to get here before he's late. *I hate when people are late.* It's one of my biggest pet peeves. That, and people who bite their nails.

I'm spacing out when there is a knock on my office door. I stand, smoothing my dress pants, and push some of my curled dark hair behind my ears. I pull open the door to be met by the sexiest man I have *ever* laid my eyes on. He's tall, much taller than my five-foot-one frame. He's wearing a fitted Henley shirt and snug jeans. His chin is covered in stubble, and his tan construction boots are covered in a fine layer of dirt.

Sexy construction worker, indeed.

I blink up at him a few times before my lips can actually process forming words. I have never had a man render me speechless just from looking at him, so color me surprised. "Mason James?" I ask, clearing my throat. He nods and I offer my hand to him to shake. "I'm Hannah Bailey, the director of *Lollipop Preschool.*"

His large hand encircles mine and the rough calluses of manual labor brush against my soft hand. I gaze at our conjoined palms and see his jagged nail beds and a gold wedding band on his ring finger. *I'm not surprised he's a nail-biter.* "Please, have a seat."

I pull my hand back and indicate a chair in front of my desk. He sits, as do I, thankful for the small amount of space between us. Word of all the James brothers being back in town has spread like wildfire. I mean, this is a small town, after all, and there's not a lot to do but gossip. The word on the street is each brother is more handsome than the last, and I've got to say, for once, the gossip is not wrong.

I moved to Falls Village a year ago, when I took this Director position, and there was a lot of gossip about the youngest James sibling, Mallory. Taylor told me over drinks one night that she cheated on her ex, Joey, with Kevin, the man she's with now. They seem like a great couple, and this town is turning around because of all the work Mallory is putting into the renovations. It's really made a world of difference and the town is starting to thrive.

She went on to tell me all about the brothers— Mason, Maxwell, and Matthew. Of course, she pulled up pictures from different social media accounts, and Mason caught my eye right away. Mason has a whole sexy lumberjack/daddy Dom vibe going on. He sits and patiently waits for me to start.

"It's nice to meet you, finally. Mallory told me there've been some family issues that have kept you away, so I'm glad we get to meet."

He gives me a quiet grunt, which I assume is 'It's great to meet you, too, Hannah.'

"Anyway, I wanted to talk to you about Amber and a few issues I've noticed."

"Issues," he says, his deep voice even as he repeats the word. *Oh my God, liquid honey is what he sounds like.* His voice reverberates through my body, each one of my nerve endings coming alive with the sound.

I clear my throat and tuck my dark, wavy hair behind my ear. "Yes, issues. She's a bright girl and picks up on the curriculum quickly, but she won't open up and has been a bit disruptive at times." He raises his eyebrow in question but doesn't say anything, allowing me to continue. "She hit another student in the class and couldn't give us a reason."

He takes a deep breath and steels his gaze on me. He has the most beautiful caramel brown eyes. "So, you called me down here because she's introverted and got picked on so she fought back?"

My mouth drops open in surprise. That is *not* the answer I thought would come out of his mouth. "Wh-no. Who told you she was being picked on? There's more going on here. I'm trained to notice things like this and to inform the parents right away. We focus heavily on social skills—"

"Ms. Bailey, the past few months have been difficult for me and my family. My wife passed away just before we moved back here."

I soften my tone and look down at his hands. He still has

his wedding band on, and he's fidgeting with it. "I heard. I'm so sorry for your loss."

He takes a deep breath and mumbles, "Thanks." He closes his eyes and scrubs his hands down his face. "Can I be honest with you?"

I nod, excited to be getting somewhere. "Yes, of course."

"Amber hates me. She's lashing out because she's angry with me and she misses her mom. I overheard her tell my brother, Matt, about the girl she hit. Amber said the girl told her she can't play with them and it hurt her feelings. She probably could have handled it better, but she's spent too much time with her uncles."

I focus on the first things he said. *What little girl hates her dad?* I want to know what he could have done to make her hate him so much. I don't know any kid, as young as her, that hates their parents. They all want love and their attention. "Why is she angry with you?"

His brows shoot up to his hairline. "I wasn't there when she needed me the most."

This is not how I thought this conversation would go. He's being so open and honest. All the rumors about Mason say he's closed off and keeps to himself. I honestly expected this conversation to end before it even began.

I open my mouth to ask more questions, but he talks first. "Listen, I'm sorry she hit that girl. I'll talk to her... or have Matt talk to her." He lowers his voice like he doesn't want me to hear him. "Maybe she'll actually listen to him."

"She's a wonderful girl, Mr. James. Please don't think otherwise. I just think she is struggling and, if it's not too bold to say, I think home life is part of the problem."

He stands suddenly and rakes his fingers through his dark

brown hair. "Stick with teaching, and I'll worry about her home life."

He gives me one more cursory glance and is out the door without another word. *Who walks away from a meeting like that? Who doesn't even stay to see their daughter?* I stand and rush to the front door, but by the time I catch up to him, he's slamming his truck door closed. He stares at me for a moment through the windshield before driving off.

I'm not sure if I should be angry with him or *sad* for him. Mallory had given me the abridged version of events when she enrolled Amber in the school. Under normal circumstances, she wouldn't have been able to enroll Amber because she's not her guardian, but after telling me what was going on, I allowed her to.

That was a few months ago. If I didn't know he had lost his wife, I would have assumed he was a deadbeat dad who didn't care. After meeting with him, seeing the worry lines that mar his beautiful face, and felt the tension rolling off him in droves, I know that's not true.

He's lost.

He needs someone in his corner to help shoulder some of the responsibility, and damn it if I don't want it to be me.

Mason James, I'm going to help fix you.

CHAPTER THREE
MASON

*H*annah Bailey. Definitely the sexiest preschool teacher I've ever met in my entire life. Her dark wavy hair and blue eyes were striking against her fair skin. *It's too soon to be looking at anyone else like that.* Isn't there an unwritten rule that you have to grieve for at least a year before you can start noticing how attractive someone is?

Find love again, Mason. Don't stop living and loving because I'm not here. Ella's words haunt me.

I park the truck at the construction site we're at today and drop my head back against the headrest, closing my eyes. Between moving out of Mallory's place into my own with my stupid ass brothers, and Amber refusing to talk to me, I've all but been gone. The town renovation is taking up more and more of my time.

Excuses.

Everything I can think of is a damn excuse because I don't know how to connect with my kid. I don't know how to comfort her or get her to talk to me. She loves her Uncle Matt, and it's been easier to push the responsibility of raising her on to him. Teddy is too young to be mad at me. All I have to do is pick him up when he cries and he smiles at me. Shouldn't Amber be too young to hate me, too?

Amber, though, is her mom through and through. Ella was always the one to hold a grudge, even if it was over something little. I swear, that woman could pull up an incident and tell me the exact date and time it happened. Of course, she could have been bullshitting me, but I never would have called her out on it. I smile at the thought of her.

"Ella, how the hell do I get through to our little girl?" I ask out loud.

Amber was always a daddy's girl. Any time she had a problem, she came to me first. If she fell and got hurt, I had to put the band-aid on and kiss it better before Ella could even look at it. I always had to read her the final bedtime story and tuck her in. That was the routine.

Since Ella's passing, I haven't done any of that. She's turned to Matt for all of it, and it's not from lack of trying, either. Every time I walk into her bedroom, her smile fades. I swear you would think I beat the child with the look in her eyes. All the sparkle fades into darkness, and it breaks my heart. To avoid seeing the hurt in her eyes, I've just... stopped.

I've distanced myself from my daughter because it hurts me too damn much to see her so sad. *Mason, you sad sack of shit, you're a grown-ass man.* It's time to man up and fix this shit. I don't want my daughter to grow up hating me, not letting me into her life.

I look at the progress on the current building. We are revamping the old mills and turning them into condos. It should help bring some of the younger crowd back into town. We've made a lot of headway in such a short amount of time.

My passenger door opens and my friend Pete Roman

slides in. "You gonna sit here all day and daydream, or are you actually planning on working today?" he jests.

"I've fucked up with Amber." I don't even bother looking at him, keeping my eyes trained on the construction site. "She hates me and is lashing out in school."

He clasps his hand on my shoulder and gives it a tight squeeze. "She doesn't hate you, man. Stop being so hard on yourself."

I look at him from the corner of my eye and frown. "She got into a fight at school because the other girls didn't want to play with her, and then she told Matt about it. She wouldn't even tell me about it." I turn to look at him head-on. "She's three. She shouldn't be hating me like this until she's thirteen and a moody teenager."

Pete chortles and shakes his head. "It's going to be fine. Take her out for ice cream or something."

I hum in thought. "Hey, do you know anything about Hannah Bailey, the director at the preschool?" Aubrey, his daughter, also goes there.

He shakes his head. "Not really. I'm sure there's gossip about her in this place; no one gets left out. Small town and all that shit."

Don't I know it. The moment I stepped foot back in Falls Village, the town was in a frenzy. Especially when news of all of us brothers being back hit. My idiot baby brother Matt is a movie star, and he's back to help draw attention to the revitalization.

Amber is attached to him like glue. She won't come within two feet of me if she can help it, but will crawl all over him. I hate that my daughter won't come to me, but turns to him instead. I need to remind myself that it could be worse. At least she has someone she can look up to, even if he's not the best role model for a little girl.

Then there's my middle brother, Max. He's decided to run for mayor here in our little town. He came in from Washington, D.C., and he is a ruthless son of a bitch. Honestly, he could be really good for this town. Mallory may have jumpstarted the idea of flipping the entire town for the better, but Max has the balls to make it happen the way he wants.

That leaves me. Everyone knows Ella passed away; I'm sure they knew before her body was even cold. That's just how these people are. Everyone is connected and everyone sees themselves as family. Until Ella came into my life, I was always more of a lone wolf. Don't get me wrong, in my younger years, I had my pick of girls. If the way some of the women in this town glance at me, I imagine I still could.

Since coming back, I've spent too many nights at my old dive bar stomping grounds, *Lucky 7*. It was easy enough to get a fake ID in high school to spend time there playing pool and drinking beer. After my stint with whiskey after Ella passed, I've stuck with pool, not drinks. I don't need Mallory to chew my ass out any more than she already did.

She's got bigger balls than I remember, that's for damn sure. Maybe Kevin was a good match for her, after all. She was never like that with Joey.

I glance at the work happening one more time before I decide to call it a day. "Pete, I'm going to leave and pick up Amber. Take her on a date for ice cream like you suggested."

He smirks and nods his head before getting out of the cab of the truck. He turns to me and says, "She'll forgive you. Just give it time and keep trying. Kids are infuriating as hell, but I wouldn't trade mine for anything. I know you feel the same, even if things are hard right now."

I don't answer him, but I don't have to. He knows he's right.

Well, *that* was a complete disaster. I run my fingers through my hair and tug at the ends as I walk through the front door. As soon as Amber sees Matt, she beams at him and gives him a big hug. Teddy squirms in my arms, and I put him down so he can chase after his sister. She lets out a shriek of delight and runs into the living room, with Teddy on her heels.

At least one of my kids doesn't hate me.

I picked Teddy up first from day care, and when I told him we were going for ice cream, his eyes lit up and he told me he wanted chocolate chip. Then we headed back to the preschool to pick up Amber. Hannah was nowhere to be seen, and that's probably a good thing, with the way I jetted out of there earlier.

I walked into her classroom, with what I hoped was a big smile, her brother on my hip, and she glared at me. Seriously, I cannot catch a fucking break with his kid. When I told her we were going to get ice cream as a family, she asked if Matt and Max were coming, too. Then, when I told her no, she asked me why not, since they are also family.

Seriously, this girl is smart as a whip. If I think I'm in trouble now, I can't imagine what she will be like as a teenager.

The entire time, Teddy was telling me about his day, and Amber sat there, licking her ice cream. She wouldn't even engage with me when I asked her questions. It was all one-worded answers. Teddy is the only one who filled the silence around us.

After dinner and a bath for the kids (something Amber

actually lets me help with, but only because Matt refuses), they are lounging on the couch watching some crappy kids cartoon that I've tuned out. Matt and Max are sitting with us, both busy on their phones.

"Some of the guys from the site are going to get drinks at *Lucky 7*, and I told them I'd pop by. You two okay to watch the kids for a bit?"

Matt's smile falters, but he nods anyway. "Sure. Don't be too late, huh?"

Amber's brown eyes meet mine and turn away just as quickly. *Seriously, what the hell do I do to get through to this girl?*

"Uncle Matty, will you read my favorite story tonight? The princess one."

I swear, this girl likes to rub it in my face that she won't let me read to her.

"You sure you don't want Dad to read it to you?" Matt tries to goad her into asking for me to do it.

"Yes. I want you to."

I sigh heavily, get up, and kiss both kids on top of the head. "I'll be back soon. Be good for your uncles."

Teddy gives me a big hug and tells me he loves me, and my dead, cold heart beats a little warmer for a second. Then I look at Amber who ignores me completely.

Maybe one drink tonight.

CHAPTER FOUR
HANNAH

*L*ucky 7, probably one of the crappiest bars I've ever stepped foot in, but it has some of the best damn wings on the planet. Seriously, I moved here from Massachusetts to take the position, and I haven't come across anything as good—ever. And that says a lot.

I'm sitting at the bar, my third glass of wine in, and I feel great. Taylor left me here a few minutes ago, feigning being tired, but I think she has a booty call she doesn't want me to know about. I invited a few other girlfriends out, but none of them could make it. So, here I am... alone at a bar.

A group of men a few stools down keep glancing in my direction. They aren't bad looking, but they don't make my skin break out in goosebumps. *No one ever has, except Mason.* That man looks like sin and dirty promises. I giggle to myself as I pick up another wing and dip it in ranch dressing. *Oh my God, seriously, this is like an orgasm in my mouth.*

The front door opens and I swear to you, I know exactly who walks in without even looking at him. Mason freaking James. The small gathering at the bar a few stools down waves him over to them. He nods his head in their direction and slowly makes his way through the crowd. He must have powers like Moses because, I kid you not, everyone steps out of his way, making room for him to pass.

The wing is halfway to my mouth when I stop and stare at him. *Did he actually get cuter from when I saw him earlier today?* Is that even a thing? One of the guys in the group, I think his name is Cole, looks at me and smirks.

"Hey, pretty girl, take a picture, it'll last longer."

Ah, yes, now I know who he is, Taylor's ex. She's complained about him before over drinks. "Not if it's of your ugly mug." *Oh my God, did I really just say that out loud?* Alcohol does do funny things to me.

He laughs, like drops his head back and belly laughs. I didn't realize I was a comedian. I smirk and lock eyes with Mason. He nods his head in greeting but doesn't say anything. Seriously, throw a girl a bone. At least say something so I can listen to your sexy timbre again.

He says something to the guys and takes a seat next to me. The bartender hands him a beer, and he takes a long drag from the bottle. I slide the plate of half-eaten wings toward him and he picks one up, taking a bite of it. We sit in silence, eating the wings. I keep looking at him from the corner of my blue eyes, hoping he will say something—anything.

I feel like this is a bad first date. I can't take it anymore. "You're not one for conversation, huh?"

I catch him smirking before he takes another sip of his drink. I glance down to see his leg bouncing on the bar of the stool. *Is he nervous?*

"I've never been big on words, no." He runs his fingers through his hair and shakes his head. A small brown lock falls over his forehead, and I'm itching to push it back into place.

"Listen, I want to apologize for today. For running out like that. Things between my daughter and me have been rough. I understand you're just trying to help."

I place my hand on his forearm. *Jesus, this man has a lot of muscle. Do not squeeze. Do. Not. Squeeze.* "Amber is a great girl. I think she's just a bit lost right now. I know you'll figure it out in time. I can tell she's a vibrant, fun-loving little girl, but she needs to come out of her shell."

He looks down at his hands, curled tight around the bottle as if it's his lifeline. Without his hold, he's going to float into the endless sea. "I don't know how to fix it, Hannah." He turns to look at me, and anything I was going to say flies out the window. The look he gives me is one of a man who has tried and failed over and over again.

My eyes soften, and I feel my entire body go lax under his gaze. This man is opening up to me. *Me.* A practical stranger who all but told him he was a shitty father earlier today. "You're lost right now, too, aren't you?"

He snorts a disparaging laugh. "Yeah, I really am," he admits quietly. "What are you doing in this dive bar by yourself? Falls Village may be a safe little town, but it still has its shitty parts, and East Brook has them.

I nod to the empty plate between us. "Best wings in town." I take a sip of my wine and smile to myself as he watches me carefully. "Besides, I wasn't alone, but she had to leave and I refuse to leave a plate of wings behind."

That earns me a smile from him. A full-tooth grin that has my panties soaked in a matter of seconds. *When's the last time I got any action?* I understand why all the ladies swooned over this man back in the day. Like I said, sin and dirty promises. His smile fades as quickly as it appeared, but I feel lucky enough to have been on the receiving end of it.

Time to be bold. No one ever solved problems by being scared. And I've got enough wine in my system to skydive without fear. "I'm going to help you," I say. He quirks his brow in response and I continue. "With Amber. I'm going to help you and her. Do you know what she told me when Mallory brought her into the school for introductions?" He shakes his head. "She told me she misses her daddy. I honestly thought it was you who passed away, not your wife."

I wince at my words. I'm pretty sure the last thing this man wants to be reminded of is his dead wife. "Sorry."

"It's okay," he murmurs. He spins the bottle between his hands, his eyes glued to it. "She said that?" He risks a glance at me, and I nod my head before downing the rest of my wine. I may be a little past the point of buzzed now. My body feels light and I don't have a care in the world. "Mallory never told me that."

"She needs a woman in her life. She's stuck hanging out with all you boys. Have you thought about dating?"

His brows shoot up to his hairline and he chuckles before shaking his head like I just told a joke. *Warning! Warning! Hannah, shut up!* "I mean, obviously not me." I lay my hand on my chest as if he doesn't know who I'm referring to. Seriously, I am never drinking alone again.

"You think dating someone will make my daughter like me again?" His tone tells me he thinks it's doubtful.

"I think you need a buffer. So, maybe not date, but like, someone to hang out with."

He shrugs and finishes his beer. "Okay."

"Okay?" I ask in disbelief. *Wow, if I knew it would be that easy, I could have just asked him to date me. Can I go back and change my request?*

"Okay. You'll be my buffer. Amber already knows you, so

it makes sense. I'm willing to try anything. And even if it doesn't work, at least I get to spend some time with a pretty lady."

"P-pretty lady? Me?" I stutter, trying to figure out what exactly is happening here. Mason James just asked me out? Well, no. I guess he asked me to hang out.

"Yeah, pretty." He smiles that full megawatt smile again, and I melt in my seat.

Hanging out with him is going to be dangerous to my ovaries. If he can make me melt with just his smile, imagine what his fingers or tongue can do. As if he can read my mind, he licks his bottom lip, his caramel brown eyes locked on mine. *Jesus, I am so screwed.*

"Okay, Mr. James, you're on. I'll be your buffer." I stick my hand out to shake on it. He looks down at it for a moment before he clasps his rough calloused fingers around mine and gives it a gentle shake. I swear, my whole hand heats up when he touches me, and it spreads through my body, settling into the pit of my stomach.

"Hmmm," he hums, but doesn't offer anything else as he drops my hand. "Give me your number, we'll plan a non-date. Are you around this weekend? Maybe we can go to dinner?"

I nod. "S-sure. Yeah, cool." *Casual, Hannah. Act casual and like this isn't affecting you at all.* I rattle off my number, and he sends me a quick text so I have his and can save it in my phone. "Well, I better get going." I toss my thumb over my shoulder toward the exit. "School day tomorrow."

I stand and wobble on my feet a little, grabbing the back of the chair to steady myself.

"How many glasses of wine have you had?"

"Not many, I'm fine," I reply, ignoring his question.

"I'll drive you home." I open my mouth to protest, and he

stares me down. "It's not open for discussion, Hannah." He helps me into my jacket then leads me outside to his truck. His hand rests on my lower back, and when I glance at his arm, he pulls back and mumbles an apology.

What have I gotten myself into?

CHAPTER FIVE
MASON

There's not a chance in hell Hannah is sober enough to drive home. I'm not even sure she's going to remember what she offered, but damn it if I won't take her up on it anyway. In a weird way, she has a point. If Amber feels she can open up to another woman, and I just happen to be around to hear it, in turn, she might open up to me.

"Where do you live?"

She's staring at me, an unasked question crossing her features. *God, she's pretty.* Her dark brown hair is pulled up into a ponytail, and her blue eyes are enhanced by the minute amount of makeup she's wearing. Her petite frame looks tiny in my truck, and when I shook her hand earlier, it felt so small in mine. I wanted to pull her body to mine and tuck her under my chin.

Classic beauty. That's the only way to describe her. Thoughts of Ella come rushing back to me, and I have to take a deep breath in through my nose and slowly push it out, calming my racing heart. *It's too soon.* It hasn't even been a year, only a few months since she passed away. I shouldn't be enjoying life while she's rotting in the ground.

I tighten my hands on the steering wheel and try to relax my shoulders. I need a massage or something. With all the manual labor and the stress of trying to take care of the kids, my muscles rock solid with tension.

Hannah lays her hand on my thigh and I tense up even more. Jesus, her hand is like a branding iron. I feel it all the way down to my bones, and my dick isn't getting the message about the mourning period. He's been like a rock, trying to break free of my jeans since I sat down next to Hannah and smelled her. She smells like the ocean on a summer's day. That's the only way I can describe it. It's not fruity, or earthy, but it is uniquely hers.

"The turn was over there," she says, gathering my attention.

"Shit, I'm sorry. Where did you say you live?"

She giggles and I damn near melt. It's the cutest fucking sound in the universe.

"Just over there on Elk Street. Number thirty-seven."

I flip around and turn down Elk Street, coming to a stop outside her place. It's cute—a small green cottage with dark red shutters and a dark wood door. It looks like it's been renovated within the past few years. We're on the edge of East Brook, but the houses on either side still appear a bit more run down.

It's easy to happen, especially being so close to the ocean. All that salty air makes the siding erode much faster than if we were inland. That's good for construction, keeps the jobs coming in. Not that we are hurting to work right now, the revitalization booming. Everyone seems to want in on it and requests for jobs are rolling in.

I slide out of my seat and jog around the front of the truck to open the door for her. I offer my hand so she can slide out. A small pang of warmth radiates through me as she accepts the help. She pulls her hand away from mine just as her feet hit the ground.

"Thanks." She looks around like she's waiting for someone to pop out of the bushes or something. "Well, good night."

"Let me walk you to your door." I can be chivalrous when needed. *Ella made sure of that.* It was one thing she was teaching Teddy to do. According to her, you can never start them too early. Boys need to know how to treat a lady and know when to walk away from one who is treating him poorly. I've actually asked Matt and Max to make sure they aren't acting like asses so Teddy doesn't pick up on the bad behavior.

Fat lot of good that's doing.

"Oh, you don't—" I give her the same look I did in the bar when she was refusing my help, and she acquiesces with a sigh. "Okay, sure."

It's a short walk up the driveway to her front door, and she fiddles with her keys. What was the movie where the guy said if she does that she wants to be kissed? *Hitch* or something like that? It was a stupid romantic comedy that Ella made me watch, but there were a few things in there that seemed to ring true.

Is that what she's waiting for? I take a deep breath and ignore the way my body craves to be close to her. It's like she's cast some sort of spell over me. I haven't been able to get her out of my mind since I met her earlier today. Then, when I walked into the bar to hang out with a few of the guys, she was there. Talk about kismet.

"I'll text you and we can do dinner this weekend. Does that work for you?"

She nods and licks her lips. I do the same, suddenly feeling very thirsty. "Do you want to come in for a drink?"

Yes. God yes. "No, I need to get home to the kids. I'm sure my brothers will be pissed if I take too much longer."

She smiles, looks to the ground, and nods. "Yeah, of course. That makes sense. Thanks for the ride home."

"Hannah, what time do you need to be at work?"

"Six-thirty, why?"

"I'll pick you up so we can get your car."

"Don't worry about it. I've already texted Taylor and asked if she could get me so I can pick it up. Thanks though. Have a good night, and give Amber a hug for me."

She unlocks the door, steps inside, and leaves me standing there, alone. Not my smoothest goodbye, but it works. *Friends, Mason.* She offered up friendship; you're reading too much into this.

Hannah: *Holy shit, Mason James is taking me on a date. Can you pick me up in the morning so I can get my car?*

I look at the text and laugh. I bet she thought she was texting Taylor. Now, the question is, do I respond to her, or just meet her here in the morning? There's no harm in spending a little more time with her. I set the alarm on my phone to make sure I can be here on time so she's not late for school, and then pocket my phone again.

Amber and Teddy are both sound asleep in bed when I walk through the front door.

"Heard you have a date with Hannah Bailey," Max says from the living room. That stupid cartoon is still playing even without the kids around. I swear those shows are so damn easy to tune out, you don't even realize you're still watching it.

"How the fuck did you hear that?" I ask, stepping into the room, my arms crossed over my chest in defense.

"Pete overheard you arranging a date for this weekend." He finally glances my way. "Good for you, man. Getting back on the saddle and all that shit. She's hot," he adds with a shrug on the end.

Fucking Pete. Just like him to say something and stir the pot. I'm sure he loved telling Max that bit of information.

"It's just as friends. She thinks having a female around will help Amber open up, and since Amber already knows her, it won't be weird. We aren't going on a date."

He nods and smirks, returning to looking at his phone. "Sure, man. Whatever you have to tell yourself. Pretty sure you're rocking a hard-on for her. Live a little, it won't kill you." His face pinches in shame. "Not what I meant, Mase."

I growl and curl my lip at him before I walk away without another word. The last thing I need to do is make waves with my brothers. They've been a huge help with the kids. I need them. Even when I don't want to admit it.

"Amber, get your shoes on. We need to go," I say, running around like a mad man. Where the hell is Teddy's jacket? I thought it was hanging up in the closet.

"Why can't Uncle Matty take me to school today?" She stays frozen on the steps, refusing to do as I've asked.

"Not now, Amber. I told you, I'm going to be taking you from now on." Teddy comes running into the room with his jacket already on. *When the hell did I do that?* I take another sip of coffee out of the travel mug and bend down in front of Amber. "Do you need help?"

"No. I can do it." She slides her tiny foot into the sneaker and pulls the Velcro strap over the top of her foot.

"Amber, do you like Miss Hannah?"

Her eyes light up at the name and she smiles as she nods. I swear this is the most genuine smile my baby girl has given me since Ella passed away. "Miss Hannah is very nice. She gives me stickers at school." She points to a smiley face sticker that adorns her pink shirt that says 'Girls and science are magic.'

"Well, she was having problems with her car last night, and I'm going to give her a ride to it. Is that okay?"

She tilts her head to the side like she's thinking about it and then nods, that smile still firmly in place. *Maybe Hannah was right after all.*

"Good. Let's go and get her."

CHAPTER SIX
HANNAH

*M*ason's truck idles outside my house, and I peek through the window as he gets out and starts walking toward the door.

Shit. Shit. Shit. Why is Mason here? I texted Taylor last night to ask if she could come to get me. Didn't I?

I open the texts from last night, and my face pales as I see I sent my message to Mason. How could I have done that? Taylor was the last person I texted...

No.

Mason texted me his number, so he was the top text message in my phone. Ugh! I really shouldn't have had that last glass of wine. I'm such a lightweight. I knew I wouldn't have a hangover if I had wine, though, and Taylor really wanted to go out. I read the message I sent and groan again. A date? Really? I lean my forehead against the solid wall and hit it a few times, reeling in my own stupidity.

He knocks on the door and I stand up straight. I look in the mirror to make sure my lip gloss is in place and take a deep breath. *No use crying over spilled milk.*

I swing the heavy wood door open and look up into his dark eyes and he smiles. "Mornin', Hannah."

I nod. "Morning, Mason. Thanks for helping me get my car, and I want to apologize for the text. I don't think we're going out on a date, not like that anyway. I know this is just a way to help bridge the gap between you and your daughter. I'm happy to help, really, I am. I don't want you to think I'm looking to date you, because I'm not."

Jesus Christ, I'm rambling and I can't seem to stop myself. At least he looks amused at my embarrassment.

"So, you wouldn't want to date me. Noted."

"Yes, I mean, no. I mean—"

"Come on," he cuts me off and jerks his head in the direction of his truck. "Don't want the kids to be late. And I'm sure you're needed to unlock the preschool.

He opens the door to the truck and I get in, still mentally berating myself for acting so lame. I turn in my seat to look at Amber.

"Morning, Amber," I say, deciding I might as well start my job as a buffer.

She smiles warmly at me. "Morning, Miss Hannah. Daddy said your car was broked."

I look to Mason who shrugs before pulling into the street. "Yeah, I had a few problems last night, but it is all fixed now and your dad was nice enough to drive me to it today." I turn my attention to the little boy in the backseat. "Hello, what's your name?" I ask him.

He giggles and looks to the ground, not wanting to meet my eyes.

"Go on, tell her your name, buddy," Mason encourages.

"Teddy," he responds quietly and giggles again.

"Fat's my brover," Amber says excitedly. "He's two. He's not big enough to go to school yet, like me. He's too little."

"I'm no little," Teddy complains and wipes under his nose.

"Yes, you are," Amber insists, and Teddy's eyes begin to water.

"Amber, enough. Leave your brother alone," Mason chastises. Amber glares at him, and I watch Mason glance in the rearview mirror at her and sigh.

"Ah, you have a three-nager," I joke.

"She takes after her mom. The same attitude and everything. I'm going to be in for a treat when she gets a little older."

He pulls up alongside my car, not hard to pick out as it's the only one in the lot, and I turn to look at the kids.

"Teddy, it was nice to meet you, and Amber, I'll see you at school." I turn to look at Mason again. "Thanks again for the ride, you didn't have to. I'll see you at the preschool soon to drop Amber off."

I slide out of the truck and get into my car. I wait for him to leave before pulling my phone out of my purse and opening a text to Taylor.

Me: *I have a story for you when I get in. Be there in ten minutes.*

"You're his what?" Taylor asks as I pour us both a mug of coffee. The kids are slowly starting to arrive, but we have a few minutes to talk before it gets too crazy. Mason hasn't shown up with Amber yet, and I want to make sure I can talk to Taylor before she gets here. I imagine anything that's said about Mason is going to make it back to him.

"Buffer. Basically, I get the ball going and a conversation flowing so he can start connecting with his daughter again."

"Interesting. And how did he come up with this idea?" She crosses her arms over her chest and smirks at me, already knowing the answer.

I'm a helper. I can't change who I am. He needs it, and I offered. Now, the way I offered... that might have been due to the almost full bottle of wine coursing through my veins. I shrug and take a sip of my coffee, buying myself another few seconds of time. "I offered."

"*Of* course, you did. It doesn't hurt he's one of the James brothers and nice to look at. I mean, he's too old for me, but," she waves her hand in front of her face. "Speak of the devil."

Mason and Amber walk through the front doors. "Morning, Amber. Mason." I nod my head at them.

"Hi, Miss Hannah and Miss Taylor," Amber says, waving at the two of us. "Is your car okay now?"

"What was wrong with your car?" Taylor asks, dragging her attention away from the little girl.

"It's fine, thank you, Amber. Mason," I turn and point to him, "gave me a ride home last night because I had one too many drinks, and then he picked me up this morning to get it."

"Really?" How interesting," Taylor says before turning and following Amber into the classroom, leaving Mason and me standing there alone.

"She wouldn't stop asking questions about you in the thirty minutes it took for us to get back here, and she thinks we went on a date last night. Can you do me a favor and pretend." He rubs the back of his neck, his t-shirt pulling across his broad chest, and looks to his feet. When I don't answer right away, he looks up and locks eyes with me. "Please. It's the longest conversation I've had with her in months."

Oh, my heart. How the hell could I refuse him?

"S-sure. Yeah, I mean, we did share wings. It could have been a date."

He gives me a half-smile. "Thanks." He looks over my shoulder at Amber and sighs. "Okay, I have to go. I'll text you later."

"Bye, Mason. Have a good day." I wave at his retreating form. It dawns on me then that Amber didn't give him a hug or kiss goodbye. Matt usually drops her off in the mornings, and she always gives him a bear hug before she runs into the classroom.

Taylor joins me again, her eyebrows raised in question. "Um, what was that about?"

I groan and shake my head at her. "I thought I texted *you* last night, but apparently, I texted him, asking for a ride to my car. Imagine my surprise when he showed up at my door."

She laughs and spills a little of her coffee. "Oh, shoot," she says as she wipes the front of her shirt.

"That's not all. I told you in that text how excited I was that Mason was taking me out on a date." I slap the palm of my hand against my forehead and groan.

"Well, if the way Amber is talking is any indication, he's excited, too."

I look to the little girl who's sitting at a table playing with a doll. She looks over at me, smiles and waves. The last thing I would want to do is break her heart.

Mason James, I hope you know what you're doing.

CHAPTER SEVEN
MASON

*A*mber actually looked somewhat happy to see me when I picked her up from school today. That's a shock in of itself, and then the whole way home, all she talked about was Miss Hannah and how nice she is. Then, it's as if she realized who I was and she clammed up again.

Seriously? Can't a guy catch a break?

Matt and Max are bickering about something when we walk in the door. I put Teddy on his feet, and he runs in the direction of the two idiots known as my brothers.

"Hey, when are you assholes going to look for your own place?" I ask, stopping them mid-argument. Teddy and Amber look up at me, and I mentally berate myself for swearing in front of them. If Ella were here, she would have smacked me upside the head and reminded me that they're little parrots and will repeat everything. "A-holes. Sorry."

"Admit it, Mase, you love having us here. It's like old times and growing up again." Matt smiles and waggles his eyebrows at me.

"You need us, so fork off," Max adds.

"What are you guys fighting about now? Can't I come home from work just once to not have you two up each other's butts?"

"We were having an intellectual—from my side, anyway—debate on who has the biggest," he pauses and looks at the kids, "eggplant."

"How the hell does one have an intellectual conversation about *that?*" I ask, dumbstruck.

"Daddy, you shouldn't say hell, it's a bad word," Amber chastises.

"Amber, can you go play in your room with Teddy?" I ask, rubbing my forehead. I just need five minutes of peace and alone time. I feel like I'm being pulled in fifty different directions.

Her lips turn down into a frown and tears start forming under her eyes. "I wish Miss Hannah was here. You're nice when she's around." Then she runs off, Teddy hot on her heels.

Both brothers turn to face me. "Miss Hannah? Isn't that Amber's teacher?" Matt asks, a sly smirk playing at the corner of his lips.

"Technically, no. She's the director of the preschool," I grumble.

"Why is Amber talking about Miss Hannah and you?" he continues his questioning.

"None of your business. She saw us talking today, that's all."

I walk away toward my bedroom before either of them can dig for more information. I sit on the edge of the bed and pull my phone from my pocket.

Me: *Amber was telling me all about you today on the ride home from school.*

I hit send before I can chicken out. God, I used to be good at talking to girls. Matt and Max like to think I wasn't lucky with the ladies when we were younger, but quite the opposite; I just knew how to keep it in my pants. Doesn't mean I didn't have the moves to make the girls fawn over me.

But I'm out of practice. I met Ella in college and she was the last woman I had to try to charm with my stunning personality and moves. That was more than ten years ago. Have things changed as far as flirting? I don't know the protocol for trying to talk to beautiful women.

Hannah: *Oh yeah? All good things, I hope.*
Me: *Only the best.*

I want to ask her on a date, I mean, out to dinner, with the kids. It's not a date if the kids are there, right? Texting her to ask feels like a copout. I click the phone icon in the corner of the screen and it begins to ring.

"Hello, Mason," she says, her voice soft and welcoming. It's soothing, hearing her say my name.

I swallow thickly and find my voice. *Here goes nothing.* "Hannah, do you have any plans tomorrow night?"

"I'm not sure, it depends on who's asking." I can't see her, but I can picture her bright smile as she teases me. I guess she's not going to make this that easy.

"Would you want to come to dinner with me and the kids? Amber was talking to me today, and then she clammed up. It was nice, having her open up to me like that, and I think having you there would help."

"Oh," she sounds a little dejected. *Does she want this to be a real date?* "Yeah, of course. Where do you want me to meet you? *Mabel's?*"

"I'll pick you up at six. How about we check out *At the Tip.* I've heard some good things about it since it opened. It has to be earlier because of the kids." *Ugh, no shit.* I really do sound like a dumb ass.

"Six it is. Looking forward to it. See you then."

"Bye, Hannah."

I smile and give myself a mental pat on the back at not fucking that up too badly. I catch a glimpse of a picture of Ella on the bedside table and my heart sinks. I shouldn't be excited about this non-date.

"She wouldn't want you to be sad and grumpy forever, Mase," Max interjects as if he can read my thoughts. I look over at him as he leans against the door frame, his arms crossed over his chest.

"I'm not grumpy," I retort back.

He snorts and shakes his head. "Whatever you have to tell yourself, but you are. Soon you're going to be telling the kids to get off your lawn. You need to smile once in a while. Shit, I think the last time I saw you smile was at your wedding."

"Well, if you ever came to visit once in a while, before Ella died, you would have seen me smile more. But you were too busy in D.C."

"Hey, asshole, you could have visited me, too, you know?" He drops his hands to his side and clenches and unclenches his fists. "I don't want to argue. I'm here now, okay? Your kids are great, just don't fuck it up like Mom did."

He walks away without giving me time to respond. And

honestly, he has a point. When Mom ran off with Craig the slimeball, Dad couldn't get out of his drunken stupor to take care of us. I was the oldest and took it upon myself to take care of Max, Matt, and Mallory until I could get out of this small town. I know that's why Mallory took my drinking after Ella passed away so hard. She had to deal with Dad the longest.

CHAPTER EIGHT
HANNAH

I've looked at myself in the mirror only about a hundred times since I came home from work and changed into a mint and navy chevron print high-low dress and paired it with my favorite pair of wedge heels. I wasn't sure what to wear for this "non-date" but still wanted to feel pretty. I touched up my make-up and even added a spritz of my favorite perfume. I've wiped my hands down the front of my dress more times than I can count, but they still continue to sweat.

I shouldn't be this nervous. It's just Mason. He's a student's father, and I'm helping him connect with his little girl. *That's all.*

Taylor: *Good luck, have fun.*
Me: *How many people are going to know about this non-date and be talking about it by tomorrow morning?*
Taylor: *I may have told Mom about it, and she may have told Olivia, the girl who bakes those cupcakes she*

*sells. I don't think she talks a lot, but she does also work
at The Hair Matrix and you know how those ladies like
town gossip.*
Me: *Great. Thanks for the heads up.*

I glance at the door when the doorbell rings. I take one
final look in the mirror, push my long dark hair behind my
shoulders, and open it. Mason is standing there in a pair of
nice jeans, a black polo top that hugs his body, and a light tan
jacket. His eyes roam over my body before finally reaching my
eyes.

"You look nice."

"Thanks." I pull a jacket on and lock up behind me. He
opens the truck door for me, like a gentleman, and waits to
close it behind me.

"Hi, Hannah. Hi, Teddy," I say, turning in my seat to look
at the kids. Teddy waves and giggles at me before directing his
attention to the small toy in his hands.

"Miss Hannah, are you and my daddy boyfriend and
girlfriend?"

I chortle. "And what makes you think that?"

"Well, Daddy said he was taking you to dinner, and only
boyfriends and girlfriends or mommies and daddies do fat,"
she says.

"That," I correct her. We've been trying to work on her
pronunciation of words in class.

"That," she says slowly, trying the word on her tongue.
"But you aren't a mommy, so you have to be Daddy's
girlfriend."

"Amber, people can go out to eat as friends. Miss Hannah
and I are friends," Mason says, looking at his daughter in the
rearview mirror."

He looks at me, his cheeks tinged pink as he mouths sorry to me. *Mason James, are you embarrassed?*

"Well, I like her, and she should be your girlfriend. Don't you like my daddy, Miss Hannah?"

I start coughing, as I was mid-swallow and have to pat my chest a few times. "Spit went down wrong," I say, trying to catch my breath. When I finally am breathing normally again, I answer. "Yes, Hannah, I like your dad. He's a very nice man." Might as well tell the truth and not sugar coat it.

"Then why don't you want to be his girlfriend?"

I don't think I've ever met a more inquisitive three-year-old in my life, and that's saying a lot. "Well, I don't know your dad very well. We only met at the beginning of this week, and it takes time before you can date someone."

"I miss my mommy," she says suddenly and starts crying.

"Shit," Mason mutters as he pulls into the parking lot just in time for not one, but two full-blown meltdowns, as Teddy decides to join the crying party.

He opens the back door and unbuckles Teddy, pulling him to his chest and rubbing his back. I help him undo Amber's car seat, and she all but flings herself into my arms. I pick her up and rub her back, humming softly in her ear.

"Boys need girls to take care of them. Daddy doesn't have my mommy anymore. She went to visit a place called Heaven. I want to go with her, but Daddy won't let me," Amber whispers as her crying subsides.

Oh, my ovaries! I want to wrap this little girl in my arms and take away all her pain. "Your dad is doing the best he can, Amber. He's trying really hard, and he loves you and your brother so much. I'll tell you what," I say, smoothing out the back of her brown hair, "let's go eat dinner and you can tell me all about your family, okay?"

She nods into my shoulder. "Okay," she says, squeezing me a little tighter.

I feel Mason's eyes on me and turn to look at him. He's still holding the little boy in his arms, but his gaze is locked with mine. Even from here, I can see all the turmoil rippling through his soul through his eyes. They are so expressive, even if his face doesn't show it. He reaches his hand out for mine, and I take it, squeezing his a little, giving him some extra strength.

"Table for four," he says to the hostess.

Dinner went about how you would expect. I did most of the talking with Amber and Teddy, and Mason was happy to sit back and watch. Mason was smart to bring some crayons and paper for the kids to entertain themselves, but that didn't give us a chance to talk too much, only a few moments here and there.

The kids fell asleep on the drive back to my place, so we finally have a few moments to ourselves. We're sitting in his truck, idling in my driveway, neither of us wanting the night to end. Well, maybe that's just wishful thinking on my part, but I don't think so. I tried to get out a few minutes ago, and he stopped me by talking.

"I appreciate what you said to Amber tonight when she was crying. She remembers Ella now, but it won't be long before her memory becomes fuzzy and she doesn't remember her at all. And Teddy?" He lets out a sad grunt. "Shit, he's probably already forgotten her." He drops his head back against the headrest and closes his eyes.

I reach my hand out to him, but, at the last second, pull it back and place it in my lap, keeping my hands in tight fists. "Mason, you're doing great. She loves you. Honestly, you don't even need me as a buffer. She's opening up to you. Give her time, you'll see."

He opens his brown eyes and stares at me. "What if I need you?" I suck in a deep, shaky breath. "Tonight felt right." He shrugs. "I like spending time with you. Would you want to go out again? Maybe we can go on a proper date, just the two of us."

Mason freaking James is asking me on a real *date! I'm doing somersaults inside while remaining completely cool, calm, and collected on the outside... I hope.*

"Are you sure you're ready for that?"

He nods. "Yeah. I'd like that. Would you want to go out tomorrow? We can go see a movie if you want."

"As long as it's not a horror movie, it sounds like a date." I lean over the middle console, lay my hand on his forearm, and kiss his cheek. "Have a good night. Text me later."

I slide out of the truck and hurry inside my house. It's cold outside, and I don't want Mason to watch me do a stupid little happy dance.

CHAPTER NINE
MASON

*W*ell, what do you know? Looks like I still have it after all. Jesus, I just asked her to go see a movie. I don't even know what's playing.

I pull out of her driveway to go home, glancing in the rearview mirror at the kids sleeping in the back. They look so peaceful, not a care in the world. I wish I could go back in time and not be such an ass to Amber. She's only this small for so long, and I don't want to lose this time with her. Before I know it, she's going to be in high school and will want nothing to do with me again.

I sigh as I park the car and sit there in silence for a few minutes. I close my eyes and drop my head back against the headrest, replaying the night in my head. Hannah was so good with the kids—not that I expected anything different. Amber was a chatterbox the whole night, and it warmed my cold heart to listen to her little voice.

Even Teddy, who normally is shy around new people, was talking to her and telling her all about his favorite toy trucks. Hannah acted like it was the most interesting piece of news she had received and asked all sorts of follow-up questions, making him smile.

I never know what to say, but Hannah, she just *gets* it. I was thrust into the role of a caregiver while I was still in high school, taking care of my younger siblings after Mom ran off and Dad was depressed and too drunk. He loved us, and he tried his best, but sometimes that wasn't enough.

Kids were always in my future, but I fully anticipated Ella to be here longer than just three short years with them. I knew the chance of her living to an old age was slim, but the cystic fibrosis kicked her ass much quicker than I expected.

I wipe the tears from my cheeks and suck in a deep breath. I clear my throat and text Matt to come help get the kids out. I want to avoid waking them if possible. I walk to the passenger side and open the back door to get Amber. As soon as she's in my arms, she wraps them tightly around my neck, her little fingers playing with the longer hair there.

"Daddy, where's Miss Hannah?" she mumbles through her sleepy haze.

"Home, baby girl. We need to get you to bed."

"You're nice when she's here," she trails off as she drops her head to my shoulder, her quiet snores in my ear letting me know she's asleep again.

Well, if that's not a kick in the nuts, I don't know what is. *Once.* I was mean to her *once* after I lost my wife—her mother —and she won't let me live it down. I look over to Matt. I know he heard her and he gives me a somber look.

"Not. A. Word," I whisper, enunciating each syllable, anger rolling off me in droves.

He holds a hand up and walks into the house with Teddy over his shoulder. Once the kids are settled in bed, I go downstairs and pour a glass of scotch. My brothers are sitting at the kitchen table, their eyes burning a hole in my back.

"Either of you dipshits have something to say?" I don't even bother turning to look at them, opting to stare at the glass of amber liquid instead. I swirl the tumbler around, watching the liquor spin round and round, getting lost in my thoughts as I wait for theirs.

"Bad date?" Max finally ventures.

I snort. "No. Great, actually. When Hannah's around, Amber really opens up. Did you know the girls in her class are mean to her because she doesn't have her hair in pretty braids?"

"Yeah, Amber told me, and I told you. Remember?" Matt says.

"No... maybe," I mumble. "I wish I had heard it from my little girl, though, instead of my baby brother. She had no problem telling Hannah when she asked if she's made friends in school." I dump the drink down the drain and swear I hear one of them sigh in relief. "I have a date tomorrow. Can one of you watch the kids for me?"

I finally turn to look at both of them, and Matt nods. "Sure, it's an early morning shoot tomorrow anyway."

I climb the stairs to my room and close the door, loving and hating the alone time all at once. I sit and then lay back on my bed, tossing my arm over my eyes. My phone buzzes and I reach into my pocket to check it.

Hannah: *Thanks again for tonight. I hope it helped some with Amber.*
Me: *It's me who should thank you. We had a great time. Pick you up tomorrow night at 6 for dinner?*

Hannah: *It's a date.*

She has no idea how happy those three words have made me tonight.

I'm so nervous about this date. I've changed my outfit at least three times, finally settling on fitted jeans, a black button-down top, and a pair of boots—nice boots. Not my ratty-ass work boots.

I keep running my fingers through my hair and wiping my hands on my jeans, unable to stop myself. Old habits die hard.

"Are you seeing Miss Hannah tonight?" Amber inquires as I walk into the living room to say goodbye.

"I am. Is that okay?"

She pauses for a moment to think and then nods. "Yup. I like Miss Hannah. Do you fink she likes flowers? You should give her some and tell her she's pretty."

I can't help the smirk that takes over my face. "That's a great idea. Thanks, baby girl."

She smiles wide at me in response. I kiss her and Teddy good night and tell them to be good for their uncle. Then I smack Matt upside the head to wake his sleeping ass up. He startles and looks around before trying to hit me back.

"Jackass," he mutters just loud enough for me to hear.

"Fat's not a nice word," Ambers chimes in.

"It's an animal—a donkey, so it's not a bad word."

"Oh, I like jackasses," she proudly announces and turns back to point at Donkey in Shrek.

I roll my eyes and glare at Matt. "Fix that. I'm going to be late if I don't leave."

I make a pit stop at the grocery store and pick up a small bouquet of wildflowers. When I pull into her driveway, I stare at them for a while, feeling like an idiot for having bought them. *What if she thinks I'm trying too hard?*

I look up in time to see her drop the curtain back in place. I turn off my truck and get out, taking the flowers with me. I ring the doorbell, but she opens it straight away as if she was standing there just waiting for me. Maybe she's as nervous as I am.

She smiles wide, instantly putting me at ease. "Amber thought you might like flowers," I offer as I hand them to her, admiring her skinny jeans and flowy top.

"Just Amber, huh?" She raises her eyebrows at me, her beautiful blue eyes never leaving mine.

"Well, I mean," I stumble, trying to make less of an ass of myself.

"Mason, I'm teasing. They're perfect. Thank you. Let me get these in some water, and we can go." She rushes to the kitchen to fill a vase with water and is back moments later. "Ready?"

I stand to the side, allowing her to step out into the cool night and lock the door behind her. I follow her down to the truck and open the door for her, mentally slapping myself for not saying something about how she looks when she first opened the door. *This was so much easier ten years ago.*

"So, what movie are we seeing?" she asks once I'm settled behind the wheel.

"That new romantic comedy with my idiot of a brother in it. He said it's good."

"Oh yeah, I've wanted to see that one. I bet the town is going crazy for it. A local boy up on the big screen and all that."

"Yeah, but I thought we could get burgers first as Mabel's. They have the best fries there," I add.

"Sure."

The whole ten-minute ride to Mabel's is quiet. Too quiet. This is terrible. This is probably the worst date she's ever been on. Why can't I just act normal? I swear, the first pretty girl who talks to me, I clam up. I guess it really is my MO. I did the same thing with Ella at first. Didn't know how to act around her. It was love at first sight for me. For her, not so much. She made me work for it, and I would happily do it again.

I'm on a date with Hannah, so stop thinking of Ella. I park the car and, before she can get out, place my hand over hers and give it a gentle squeeze.

"I don't know how to do this." I wave my hands between us to enunciate my point. "Date. I haven't had to impress a girl in a long time. Don't judge me based on this night, okay?"

She gives me a warm smile. "Stop trying so hard and just be you. Let's agree that we are just hanging out as friends. Three dates minimum, and if you want to go further, we can discuss it then. If not, we can stop this, but I will still be there to help you and Amber. How's that?"

CHAPTER TEN
HANNAH

*O*h God, the way he's looking at me right now makes it seem like I have six heads. Did I already blow my chance with him? Did I even have a real chance, to begin with?

He lets out a deep breath as his shoulders relax. "Yeah, I'd like that."

I can do that, right? Three dates as friends, nothing more. I'll start now and offer to go Dutch and pay for my half of the evening. "Perfect, just friends then. Let me pay my way for the night."

He laughs. Like, full, deep belly laughs at me. *I didn't realize I was so humorous.* I narrow my eyes at him, waiting for him to stop laughing and explain exactly why I'm so funny. This isn't a date; therefore, I'll pay my own way.

"Hannah, you're not paying." I open my mouth to protest and he cuts me off. "I asked you. Doesn't matter if we aren't labeling this a date. You're not paying your way." He looks out the windshield at the bustling diner. "Besides, this is a small town. Can you imagine the scandal if these old bats found out you and I were out and I didn't pay?"

I purse my lips trying to picture it and nod in understanding. Small towns talk. Mason returning after the death of his late wife was already the latest gossip on the streets from the locals. Since the revitalization, there are more tourists coming to visit, so I hear less talk when I'm out than I used to.

He gets out and jogs around the front of the truck to open the door for me and help me to the ground. He holds his arm out, allowing me to walk ahead of him, and places his hand on the small of my back. Warmth radiates through my entire body at his touch, and I have to keep myself moving forward. I gasp and he pulls it away just as quickly as if I've scorched his flesh.

He pulls the door open for me and leads me to an empty booth, waiting for me to sit first. *So much for this not being a date.* This man is the epitome of chivalrous. I'm not even sure if he's cognizant of his actions, and that thought warms me through. I slide into one side, and he takes up space across from me. Spreading his long limbs out, he takes up as much space as possible.

I don't even need to look at the menu. I order the same thing every time I come here because it's just that good. Bacon cheeseburger with extra pickles, fries with a side of ranch, and a cherry cola. For a hot second, I contemplate ordering a salad, like I did last night, but this isn't a date, and I don't have to pretend. Besides, why go to a restaurant and order a salad? I can make that at home if I want it.

Instead, I take the time to gaze at Mason as he peruses the menu. His dark hair is slightly unkempt as if he was running his fingers through it before picking me up. The stubble on his jaw is short and well-trimmed, and my mind drifts to thoughts of what it would feel like between my thighs. I'm sure I would remember him there the next day. My cheeks burn and I touch my cool hands against them, warding off the heat.

"Aren't you going to look at the menu?" He puts his menu down and glances at me.

I shake my head. "I get the same thing every time I come here." Samantha, my usual waitress, comes over and smiles warmly at us. I don't miss her ogling Mason before talking to me. *I wonder if she knows him from school.* I think she grew up here. I'm pretty sure it's bad that my first thought when I noticed her doing that was "back up, bitch," right?

"Hey, Hannah, the usual?" I beam at her and nod. She looks to Mason, biting her lip and smiling. "And what can I get you?"

"Well, apparently, Hannah knows what's good here if she gets the same thing every time. I'll take that." He hands the menus to her, and she leaves us alone.

"Don't you even want to know what it is?" I ask, dumbfounded. Why would he do that?

"Nope. The waitress knows your order, which means you get it often enough. If it's that good, I'm sure I'll like it."

I place my elbows on the table and lay my chin on the back of my folded hands. "You don't seem like the type of man who lives on the edge."

No. From what I know of Mason, from hearing town gossip and for the little bit of time I've spent with him, he plans everything. He's probably meticulous about every aspect of his life. The only thing I'm sure he couldn't have planned for is the death of his wife, and that's why he's so hard up when it comes to his kids. I know he loves them. Dinner last night proved that. He's great with them, but he's also lost.

I'm sure returning here wasn't part of his life plan. I don't know many people who grew up here that willingly come back —except for the James kids. Although, I believe Mallory forced them to come back for a while. *I wonder how long he plans on staying here?*

"I can be adventurous," he quips. He takes a sip of his cherry cola and puts the glass back on the table, staring at it. "Cherry Coke. Not bad," he adds, nodding his approval.

When did Samantha give us drinks? I really need to get out of my own head and focus. He's going to think I'm an airhead if I keep zoning out.

"Adventurous, huh?" My smile takes over my whole face. "Tell me the craziest thing you've ever done?"

He rests his head in his palm and taps the side of his stubbled cheek with his index finger. "Hmm," he hums as he continues to think. "Mile high club on the way to Aruba."

I lift my eyebrow in surprise. I definitely was not expecting that to be his answer. His caramel eyes sparkle, and I can only assume he's remembering it. It's so messed up that his answer makes me jealous.

"How about you?" he asks, waiting for me to answer.

Now, the thing about me is, I haven't dated much. I'm not a virgin, by any means, but I'm close to it. I've always thought one shouldn't sleep around, but wait for someone special. Too bad I came to this conclusion after giving up my V-card in high school. Prom. So typical. He was my boyfriend and we were going to be together forever. We had known each other since birth and dated since middle school. Winter Springs sweethearts are who we were known as.

We lasted exactly one month into Freshman year of college before I dumped him for cheating on me in his dorm. We went to different schools, and I came home for a long weekend to surprise him. Turns out I was the one who was surprised when I pushed open the door to his dorm room to

find him dick deep in some skinny blonde. He made me feel
like a fool.

I have exactly two men under my belt, including my loser
ex. The next guy, Josh, I dated for a while before I moved here
and he didn't want to come. He was nice enough, easy on the
eyes, but I should have known it wouldn't last when he started
talking about a job in New York. Also, when we had been
dating for almost a year, and every time I brought up the idea
of living together, he would quash it.

"I'm not that adventurous, hence why I always get the
same thing. Plus, I mean, it's amazing." Such a cop-out answer.
I can tell he thinks so, too, with the confused look on his face.

"Everyone's done something they find crazy. Name something," he urges for a different answer.

I take a moment to think, and gasp, a forgotten memory
coming back to me. "I've sent nudes."

He smirks, and I swear my heart stops. It's a mixture of
promises of pleasure and sin. I can see the wheels turning in
his head, and I know he's totally thinking about it. His eyes
roam down my body, stopping on my pert breasts before traveling back up.

"Lucky man."

CHAPTER ELEVEN
MASON

*W*hoever the man was that got those pictures of her, he is one lucky S.O.B. Hannah, from what I've been able to tell, has an amazing body. From the few times I've seen her, she doesn't like to put the goods on display. Even at *Lucky 7*, she was dressed nicely, unlike some of the other women there that night.

Innocent.

Pure.

That's what I think of when I look at Hannah Bailey. So, hearing her say she's sent nudes to someone before seems to have come from left field. *I wonder what body part was on full display...*

"It was my ex, from high school," she adds as her cheeks flush a beautiful pink. She clenches her jaw, and I notice the twitch of a scowl on her lips.

"I take it the relationship didn't end on good terms?"

"Unless you consider walking in on him balls deep in another woman, good, then no, it didn't."

I flinch and a low whistle passes my lips. "He was an idiot to have lost you."

She shrugs and looks into the diner at the other tables. Only half of the tables are full, but I can feel the stares coming from some of them. I recognize Evelyn Waters, Lenny Waters' mother, sitting with a few friends. She's not known for her gossip, but I'm not familiar with the women she's with. And then there's Mable, the owner of the diner, and while I haven't seen her tonight, I'm sure she's lurking somewhere. She'll tell anyone who will listen about our date.

Not a date.

She lays her hands down on the counter and fidgets with the paper she tore off the napkin, avoiding my gaze. I want to look into her cerulean eyes to read her thoughts. Her eyes speak volumes where words fail. As if she can read my mind, she looks up at me. Love, loss, pain, and relief are all reflected back. So many emotions she carries for this man who broke her heart.

"It was a long time ago. No use being upset about it now. At least he didn't show them to anyone."

Samantha comes by with our burgers. I've got to hand it to Hannah; her choice was on point. A bacon cheeseburger with fries. You can never go wrong with that.

"Nice choice," I point at the burger in front of me as she reaches for the ketchup.

Her warm smile begins to melt the icy walls I've built around myself since losing Ella. I shouldn't be here. I shouldn't be enjoying the company of another woman. It's too soon. *She wouldn't want you sad and grumpy forever.* Max's words come to the forefront of my mind, plaguing me. I know he's right, but it feels like I'm cheating. Even Ella told to me to move on before she passed away.

I glance down at my wedding band. The dull gold stands out against my tanned skin. I haven't had the courage to take it off yet, so instead, I pretend. Not that there's any reason to, except for my own sake. Everyone in this town knows I'm single, so it's not like I can use it to ward off unwanted advances. Which, by the way, have been several.

I swear the stories of us James boys must be widespread because women look at the three of us with stars in their eyes. Matt, I can see because of him being a celebrity and all that, but not Max or me.

"Mason," Hannah says. I look up at her and try to smile. "We don't have to do this if you don't want to."

"Can I tell you something?" I venture. She nods, pushing a fry into her mouth. "I like you."

"I like you, too, Mason." That pretty blush returns to her cheeks.

"But I feel like it's too soon. I want to do this, I want to keep seeing you, but I feel like I'm cheating on her. She hasn't been gone long enough for me to start falling for someone again."

She reaches out for me, and I let her place her small hand over mine. "Mason, I told you, we don't have to rush anything. We can just be friends. I don't want you to feel pressured into anything you aren't ready for." She takes a deep breath, and my heart stills with her next words. "Will you tell me about her?"

I shake my head, lean back into the seat, and plunge my fingers through my brown locks. I push my breath through my nose and try to come up with the best way to explain my reasoning. It's not that I don't want to talk about Ella; it's just that I don't want to talk about Ella with *her*. I don't want her to feel like she's coming in second place. It's hard enough to compete for someone's affections without adding a dead person into the mix.

"No. Not tonight. Tonight, I just want to enjoy our time getting to know one another." I pick up my burger and take a bite out of it. "Damn good choice," I announce, and she beams at me.

I walk through the front door and find Matt sleeping on the couch. I've got to hand it to my baby brother; his acting skills aren't bad. Normally, I wouldn't go see a movie called *Male Delivery*, but it wasn't as horrible as it sounded. Hannah seemed to enjoy it, and I will deny it until I'm blue in the face, but so did I. The only thing I didn't care for was seeing my brother naked—well, almost naked—on screen. Hannah didn't seem to mind ogling him, though.

I kick him in the leg gently to wake his lazy ass up. He takes a deep breath and smiles at me. "Hey, how was the movie?"

"It didn't suck as bad as I thought it would, although I would prefer to not see you practically naked on the big screen. Seeing you normal-sized is bad enough."

"Bet Hannah enjoyed seeing me naked, though." He wiggles his eyebrows and gives me a shit-eating grin when I scowl back at him. "Kids are asleep. I take payment in the form of Venmo or cash."

"How about you're living under my roof for free like a squatter, and I don't owe you shit?"

He groans. "Will you hurry up and get laid already? You need to get your rocks off so you can stop being so fucking cynical. It's such a mood killer."

"I don't need to get laid." *Lies, I really do need to get laid.* "I need to get my kids to like me again."

He sits up, putting his feet on the floor. "Well, it's a good thing you're dating Hannah then. Amber was talking about her all night, going on about how she's so nice and pretty."

"We aren't dating, jackass. We're friends, that's it."

If I tell myself that enough times, maybe I'll actually start to believe it. Three dates... not dates, is what we agreed on. Tonight was so damn easy with her. I'm nervous until she's with me, then it's like the world tilts on its axis and everything is right. Ella is the only woman I've ever felt that with. Like two magnets, we were always drawn to one another. I feel that now with Hannah.

"Okay. Whatever you have to tell yourself. I'm going to bed. When you jack off, try to keep the noise level to a minimum. I have another early shoot and need my beauty sleep." He pats my shoulder as he passes by.

I go around the house, making sure all the doors and windows are locked tight for the night and shutting off all the lights. I check on the kids, kissing both their sleeping heads and tucking them in tight. Teddy kicks his blankets off two seconds after I pull them up, and I shake my head, a smile gracing my lips.

Finally, I'm alone in my room, and the only person I can think of is Hannah. Throughout the entire movie, I was hard as a rock, and even my naked-ass brother couldn't make it go away. Having her so close was torture. I could see her, smell her, hear her, but I couldn't touch her. I wouldn't allow myself to. She told me three dates, and that's what it's going to be. I will hold out for three dates, but after that, I make no promises.

I shuck my clothes and grab myself through my boxers. As much as I don't want my brother to be right, there's not a chance in hell I'm going to be able to sleep with this raging hard-on. I lay back on my bed, close my eyes, and picture the seductive preschool teacher, wishing she was here to lend a hand.

"Daddy, do you fink fat you and miss Hannah are going to get married?" Amber asks me while eating breakfast Wednesday morning, the milk from her bowl of cereal dripping down her chin. It's been four days since my *not* date with Hannah, and we've texted and talked every day. When we aren't talking, I can't get her out of my damn mind. Which, at the site, isn't a good thing. I've already almost face-planted in a hole dug for foundation and almost walked into a pile of wood. Pete gave me shit for it and told me to get my dick wet already. *Asshole.*

"I told you, Amber, Miss Hannah and I are just friends." I wipe her face, hoping to not have to change her shirt again this morning.

"She's pretty, and you need a mommy to take care of you."

"Oh yeah? And Teddy, what do you think of that? Do you like Miss Hannah?" I ask my little boy.

"Yes." He giggles and puts the spoon of cereal in his mouth.

"Well, Miss Hannah and I are getting to know one another right now. I'm not going to marry her yet."

Max comes into the kitchen like a zombie, eyes half-lidded as he reaches for the coffee pot. "Who aren't you marrying yet?"

"Miss Hannah," Amber proudly announces.

He fills his mug, takes a sip of the black liquid, and turns to look at me. "*Yet*, huh?"

I ignore him. "Come on, kids, I've got to get to work. Finish up breakfast and brush your teeth."

"Mason and Hannah sitting in a tree..." Max sings as he fades into a hum, walking out of the room. He's lucky I don't have time to deal with him; otherwise, he'd be getting a swift kick in the nuts.

CHAPTER TWELVE
HANNAH

The rumble of Mason's truck echoes through my office, and I can't help the school girl squeal that bubbles up inside me. Ever since our date on Saturday night, we've been talking or texting. Every time his name lights up my phone, I can't help but smile and want to respond immediately. He probably thinks I'm some sort of a stalker, always responding so quickly.

I stand by the door with Taylor, like we always do, greeting the kids and the parents as they walk through the double doors, excited to start another day of learning and fun with their friends. Mason walks through the parking lot with Amber's hand in his. I don't know if I'm imagining it, but as soon as he sees me, I swear, his face lights up.

Amber waves excitedly at me and starts pulling on Mason's hand to make him walk faster.

"Good morning, Amber," I say as they walk through the doors together.

"Guess what, Miss Hannah?" she asks excitedly.

I crouch down to be able to look her in the eyes. "What?"

"Daddy needs a new mommy, and I want you to be it."
She's bouncing on her toes, her eyes shining with glee.

Mason, on the other hand, groans and covers his face with
his large palm, then focuses his attention on his daughter.
"Amber, I told you this morning, Miss Hannah and I are
friends." He looks at me and mouths 'sorry'.

"On that note, how about you and me go say good morning
to some of the other students. Huh, Amber? We can leave Miss
Hannah and," Taylor pauses and smirks, "*Daddy* to talk for a
minute." She sticks her hand out for Amber to grab.

"Bye, Daddy." Amber waves at him as Taylor leads her
into the classroom.

I can feel the heat settling in my cheeks as I wait for the
embarrassment to pass. I may have called him *daddy* once
when I was talking about how sexy he is and all the naughty
things I want to do with him. Taylor, of course, knows this and
is determined to make my life a living hell for it. Can you
blame a girl, though? With the bulging biceps, rugged appearance, and scruffy jaw, he begs to be called Daddy... and not by
his children.

"Jesus," I mumble as Mason chuckles. Taylor's infliction
on the word is not lost on him.

"Sorry about Amber. She's been on this kick of there
needing to be a mom around to take care of us boys. Since
we've been hanging out, she has the idea in her head that it's
going to be you. I keep trying to tell her it doesn't work that
way, and that we're friends."

My smile falters, only slightly, and I screw it back in place
before he notices. *I hope anyway.* "Totally fine, I get it."

"Hey, so, I wondered if you were around tonight? Maybe
we could do non-date number two?"

I put my hand to my chest and feign shock. "You want to

hang out with me three times in a week? I must actually be cooler than I thought, Mason James."

"When did I ever say you weren't cool?" He smiles and I swear his eyes light up as well. *That seems to be something new...*

"What did you have in mind?"

"Well, since we've already done a movie non-date, and dinner, I was thinking we could take a drive up the shoreline and look at the stars."

Wow. That sounds so romantic. I'd be a liar if I said that didn't sound like a great idea, and I would very much enjoy looking at the stars. It's one of my favorite past times. For some reason, my eyes skirt down to his fingers, and I see the gold band still firmly planted on his fourth finger.

It's not that I expect him to take it off right away; he was married to her for a long time, and I know he's still grieving, but I would like to not have the reminder that I'm second best. I shrink down a minuscule bit but keep the smile firmly planted on my face. We are still in a trial period, so I have no right to ask him to take it off. He doesn't owe me anything.

"That's going to be a late night, isn't it?" My brows raise to my hairline in surprise.

He rubs the back of his neck, dipping his chin to his chest. "Yeah, I know." He lowers his voice even more. "I wanted to be able to spend some time with you, away from prying eyes and ears. We can wait until this weekend if that would be better for you, but I promised Teddy and Amber we would go for ice cream and to the park.

"You can say no. I won't be offended. It is a school night, after all."

This man has no idea how quickly I want to say yes. How desperate I am to spend time with him. After our movie date on Saturday, he has been running through my mind the past four days, non-stop. I even had to take out my old friend Sven for a play session. The silicone definitely isn't as great as the real thing, but beggars can't be choosers.

Even if it wasn't Mason, and I have *no* clue how big that man is, I can tell you it didn't stop me from coming around it—hard. Of course, the scrumptious *daddy* in front of me was my point of focus. Mainly his rough, calloused hands and his beard. Both of which I pictured between my thighs, bringing me to pleasure. Even now, being around him causes my belly to tighten and wetness to form between my legs. I try to shift my weight, hoping to ease some of the pressure building there.

"Hannah? Are you still with me?" Mason waves his hand in front of my face. *Oh shit!* Talk about embarrassing. I completely spaced out in front of him, too busy with my fantasy of having his hands roam my body, bringing me to pleasure. *I really need to get laid.*

"I'm so sorry, Mason. I haven't had enough coffee and had a long night." I swear, I wasn't just imagining you naked and pleasuring me. "You know what? Let's do it." *Yes, let's do it. That's not a double meaning at all.*

"Great. I'll pick you up tonight at nine. I promise to have you home before midnight. Don't want you to turn back into a pumpkin, after all." He grins from ear to ear, and I smile along with him. I glance over my shoulder at Amber and sigh.

"It's going to take more than a few days, Mason. She will come to you when she's ready."

He nods and is out the door without another word.

"Is *Daddy* going to take you for a ride tonight?" Taylor asks, a wicked gleam in her eyes.

I roll my eyes and ignore her. "Don't you have a classroom of kids to be attending to?"

Nine on the dot, I hear the rumble of his truck outside my house, and I don't even give him a chance to cut the engine. I'm jogging down the sidewalk as soon as he pulls to a stop. I expect it to be chilly, so I've traded my dress for a pair of jeans and a hoodie. I get into the truck and smile as he's wearing the same.

"Great minds," I say pointing to his sweatshirt. "So, where are we going?"

"It's a surprise," he comments and doesn't add anything else. I give him another minute to add to his statement, but he remains tight-lipped.

Ah, yes, the man of few words is back. I settle into my seat, opting for silence instead of trying to fill the void. There's something relaxing about being in a car and having *nothing* to listen to but the roar of the engine and other cars as they pass. Almost hypnotic. I zone out, watching the darkened streets and trees blur as we pass them.

He finally slows and turns down an unmarked road. There are no lights, sans his headlights, and it's a little creepy. In a horror movie, this would be where the characters get killed. Narrow road, woods on either side, and nothing and no one for miles.

I swallow thickly, trying to get my bearings as we pull out into a clearing.

He cuts the engine and turns to look at me. "Nervous?"

I worry my bottom lip between my teeth as I glance at him. "That depends. Are you planning on murdering me out here?"

He smiles at my joke and shakes his head. "Nope, just wanted to watch some stars. Come on."

When I step out, the cool salty air tickles my senses as the sound of the waves crashing to shore fades into the night. *In and out.* I time my breaths with the breaking of each wave, closing my eyes to picture the darkened shoreline below us. We're miles from lights, but I walk to the edge of the cliff, leaning against the derelict wooden barrier to peer into the depths below. Off in the distance, I see a lighthouse, the light spinning to warn incoming boats of the rocks. It must be the one in Falls Village.

I meander back to the truck in time to watch him lower the tailgate and spread a blanket out in the bed of the truck. There are two thermoses leaning against the side of the bed. It seems he's thought of everything tonight. He jumps down and stands in front of me.

"Can I help you up?"

I nod. His large hands grasp my tiny waist, and he lifts me like I weigh nothing, placing me on the hatch. Sitting here, we are almost the same height, and I stare into his eyes, not wanting to look away. He licks his lips, and I follow his actions, wetting my own. He's captivating and has me under his spell. I lean closer, my body yearning for his, my face only inches from his.

I haven't known Mason that long, but I'm quickly coming to realize I *crave* him. He tightens his hands on my waist, and until that moment, I hadn't realized he was still touching me.

"Three dates, right?" I ask, my breathy voice breaking the silence between us.

He drops his hands and takes a step back, the spell between us broken. I hate myself for doing that. I don't want to wait. I want to feel his lips on mine, feel his hands roaming my body, and have him pressing himself between my thighs. I *want* Mason James... but I wonder if he's ready for me?

CHAPTER THIRTEEN
MASON

Three dates, right? Those words were like a bucket of ice water being doused over me. She's right. We agreed to three dates. Whether that's for her benefit or mine, I'm not sure. I know we should be taking things slow, but it's so damn hard. The more time I spend with her, the stronger the urge to have her is.

Think of the kids.

Amber and Teddy are already in love with Hannah, so I know if she wants more that I won't have an issue with the kids. My jackass brothers have been giving me shit since the first time I took her out. Especially because I took the kids with me. Even explaining it was to help bridge the gap between Amber and me didn't work. *They* are who I'm worried about. I know they want to see me get back in the saddle, but I don't want to tell them any more than I have to because they will eat that shit up.

"Yeah, three dates." I drop my hands and climb into the truck bed, sitting next to her. Both of us lean back against the cab and look up toward the dark sky. The trees around us obstruct some of the view, but other than that, it's a perfectly clear night. I hand her one of the thermoses, and she looks down at it. "Hot cocoa."

Her bright smile lets me know I made the right choice in bringing it. She opens the top and grasps the sides as the steam travels up into the cool night air. I watch her from the corner of my eye as she takes a sip, humming in appreciation.

"This is good. Swiss Miss?"

I snort and shake my head. "Nope. Homemade." I may not be the best cook in the world, but I know how to make a few things. I'm a firm believer in a good cup of cocoa, especially when the weather gets cold. Ella always bought the powdered stuff, but I decided one day to surprise her and make it myself. The powdered stuff was never seen in our house again.

"Impressive. A hot cocoa connoisseur." She takes another sip and closes the top, keeping the warm drink from getting cold. "So, how did you find this place?"

I lay back, stretching my arms up over my head, propping my head on my hands. "High school. I used to come out here for some alone time when things at home got too... *real*. I found it one night as I was driving around."

I glance at her out of the corner of my eye and see her grimace. Her lips move a fraction as if she's talking to herself. She shakes her head and slides down, so she's lying next to me. The floral scent of jasmine wafts toward me as the wind carries her scent. Her body is so close to mine that, even through our layers of fabric, I can still feel her body heat, my body instantly reacting to it.

Thoughts of jacking off to the memory of her filter through my mind as my dick stiffens in my jeans. I stave off the urge to shift and readjust myself. The more I think about it and her, the tighter my jeans get. *Thank God it's dark and she can't see me well.* We lay in silence, both of us looking up at the stars, listening to the ocean waves crashing below us.

"You know, you're the first woman I've ever brought here."

Her quiet gasp of surprise makes me smirk. It tells me everything I needed to know about what was going on inside her head. She was wondering how many other women I've brought here. None. Not even Ella. We didn't spend much time in Falls Village—hardly any, in fact. When we were in town, we were visiting Dad or Mallory and the days were always so busy.

Besides, this isn't a place you can come to during the day. It's only good for stargazing, and usually during the summer months, when we would come to town, the sky wasn't great for viewing. Too many clouds or too much light pollution always dimmed the beauty of this spot. Once the nights start getting cooler, it's worth it. And tonight, it's definitely worth it.

I've been thinking of driving out here just to get away since I moved into my own place, but as soon as the thought enters my mind, something comes up. Either I have to deal with the kids, or my brothers have created some sort of mess I feel responsible to help clean up. I've been looking after all of them for so long, even living in Portland, that it's hard to stop. Old habits die hard.

"This can be your special place, too, if you want. Just don't go around town telling everyone about it; otherwise, we'll never be able to spend time here."

"Cross my heart, I won't tell a soul."

I reach my hand down and intertwine our fingers. She doesn't pull away and I smile. My entire being feels warm and *alive.* I haven't had that feeling in at least a year. I want to roll to my side, take her beautiful face between my hands, and kiss her breathless. I have never wanted to kiss someone as badly as

I want to kiss Hannah Bailey. Her skin looks soft, and her lips look full and delectable. I'd bet my left nut she's a good kisser. The pulse in her neck is fluttering like crazy. Her breath comes out in small pants, barely noticeable, but I'm so in tune with her I can't help the observation.

"Will you tell me a secret?" she whispers as if the sound of her voice will desolate the stillness surrounding us.

A secret. I have so many. Well, maybe not secrets, but memories. My past. Moments I'd all but forgotten, and some I will never be able to. I'm broken. I broke once, after Mom left, and I was a shell of myself until Ella walked into my life. She picked up the pieces, one by one, and showed me what life could be like if I opened up and let her in.

I never considered myself a romantic until I met her. A one girl at a time guy, sure. I never slept around like my brothers, but I also didn't know how to *love*. She taught me it was okay to give someone my heart, to *trust* someone else to take care of me. That I didn't have to do it all alone.

I've had time to reflect. *Lord, have I had time.* People say you'll never find the answers you want at the bottom of a bottle. I didn't find the answers I wanted, but I sure as hell learned what I needed.

"My mom walked out on us when I was in high school, and my dad became a drunkard after. I've been taking care of my family for what feels like my entire life, but I don't know how to take care of my own kids. I feel like I'm fucking it up at each turn. I'm... lost."

She's quiet. Too quiet. She asked for a secret, and I told her one of the more intimate things I could think of. Say something. *Anything.* Moments tick by, the tension I feel waiting for her response stifling me.

"Mason?" Her voice cuts through my thoughts.

"Yeah?"

She gasps suddenly, the noise so loud in comparison to everything around us that I startle. "Did you see that?" She points skyward, her smile overtaking her features. I shake my head, unable to stop the Cheshire cat grin. *And this is why I love this spot so much.* "A shooting star!"

She sits up, frantically searching the deep blue sky above for more twinkling, shooting stars.

"Make a wish," I whisper to her. My voice comes out huskier than I mean it to, but I can't stop how she's making me feel. If I could, I would climb on top of her and press her down against the cold metal under us. Let our tangled bodies warm each other up. My dick presses even harder against the zipper of my jeans, begging to be let out, knowing how warm Hannah would be.

I watch her close her eyes, her face still turned up toward the sky, smiling. A moment later, she tilts her head back down and opens her eyes to look at me. I sit up, resting my weight on my hands. "What'd you wish for?"

She puts her index finger to her lips and cocks her head to the side like she's thinking. "I can't tell you or it won't come true, and I *really* want this one to come true."

I take a sip of the cocoa and ponder her statement, trying to figure out what wish could be that important to her. Was she wishing for a million dollars? Or maybe she was wishing for a cute dress she's seen at the store or something insignificant.

"What if I tell you what I wished for?" I didn't even see the damn shooting star, too wrapped up in my thoughts and looking at her pretty face to notice much else. Besides, who needs stars when I've got the most beautiful girl in town lying next to me, talking about mundane things?

Doing this, being here with her tonight—makes me happy.

It seems like the only times I can remember actually smiling, or feeling like the weight of the world is off my shoulders lately, is when I'm in her presence. She calms the raging monster inside of me. Heals my wounds. The magnetic pull drawing me to her is magnanimous. Every morning, when I drop Amber off at school, we spend a few moments talking. And every day, it gets just a little harder to leave to go to work.

That's why I was desperate to see her again tonight. The void I have in my heart from Ella's passing gets filled when I'm with Hannah. I don't feel so alone. My problems aren't mountains anymore, but become foothills. It's happened so fast, and yet, it feels as if it's taken us years to get here, even though it's been mere weeks.

"If you tell me, it won't come true."

God, she's cute. "I'm not that superstitious. I believe we can make our own wishes come true. It's not impossible; it might just take a bit longer to get there."

She breathes deep and closes her eyes. Her brows draw in and her lips move as if she's saying the quote out loud but to herself at the same time. "I love that."

She settles back down, looking up at the stars. We lay like this, not talking, barely touching for so long her eyes start fluttering closed. Her long, dark eyelashes fan across her soft cheeks as her breathing evens out. I extend my arm out and help situate her so her entire body turns into mine, her head resting on my shoulder.

I never did tell her what I wished for, and as much as I said I'm not superstitious, I don't want to risk having this one not come true. Especially because, after she closed her eyes, I witnessed my own shooting star.

I wish that we were already past three dates and I could stop pretending that I just want to be friends with her. I can stop pretending that she's not the highlight of my day, or that she doesn't consume my thoughts. Her breathing is deep and even against my shoulder, and I tilt my head down to lay a gentle kiss on top of hers.

I don't want this night to end. I want to stay here with her cuddled into my side. And in the morning, I want to take her to breakfast and forget all of my responsibilities. Just for one day, I don't want to be "dad". I don't want to be the boss. I just want to be Mason James, spending time with the woman that's turned my life upside down.

But I can't.

I can't leave my life behind in favor of being irresponsible, no matter how much I want to. I glance at my watch. We've been out here for about two hours now. As much as I don't want to end the night, we have to. I need to get her home, and I need to get back to the kids. We both have work tomorrow.

"Hannah," I whisper, pushing some of her dark hair away from her face. She stirs and buries her face further into me. I chuckle quietly, my body shaking hers. "Hannah, we gotta get back. You gotta wake up."

She sucks in a deep breath and pulls away from me, wiping her mouth. "Sorry. I guess I'm more tired than I thought I was. What time is it?"

"Getting close to midnight. Come on, let me get you home."

I help her into the truck and toss the blanket and thermoses in the back of the cab. It doesn't take us long to get back, especially with no cars on the roads. Begrudgingly, I pull into her driveway and put the truck in park.

"Mason, what happens after three dates?" She turns her head, catching my gaze. I can't read her expression, but if I had to guess, I'd say she looks worried.

"Hmm. Well, I guess that depends on you."

She shakes her head, her expression doleful. "It depends on *you,* Mason. I know what I want." She looks out the window to her dark house. "Thanks so much for tonight. I promise to keep your special place a secret. Thanks for sharing it with me, though." I unclick my seatbelt, and she puts her hand on my thigh.

"Get home. You don't need to walk me up. I'll see you tomorrow."

Tomorrow. Can I get the third date over with now so I can stop pretending?

CHAPTER FOURTEEN
HANNAH

*D*eath warmed over.

That's what I feel like this morning. I was out way too late with Mason last night, and I'm in desperate need of coffee. I fill the liner with coffee and pour the water into the top of the machine, hoping for some miracle that it will be ready in less than five minutes. Which, by the way, is doubtful. We need a new one because this one takes too long to brew.

I was surprised I could even drag myself out of bed, especially because I only got about four and a half hours of sleep. It took me a long time to wind down from my date with Mason last night. I can't even say *not date*. That was a date through and through.

It was perfect.

The cocoa, the stars, and the company. I'll never forget that place. It was... magical. There is no other way to describe it, as lame as that sounds. The sound of the waves below us, trees surrounding us, and the stars above us all lead to a cumulative feeling of happiness. There are very few places I've been to that elicit that kind of feeling from me, and I never thought it would be in Falls Village. Well, if we were even still within the town limits.

Taylor arrives, and on her heels is Mason. And he's holding a coffee cup in one hand, and Amber's hand in the other. My smile spreads across my face, and I'm unable to stop it.

"I'll pretend that smile is for me," Taylor whispers as she walks past me.

"Mornin', Miss Hannah," Amber announces proudly.

I squat down to her level. "Good morning, Amber. Why don't you put your stuff in the classroom with Miss Taylor."

"Bye, Daddy." Amber waves at him, leaving us alone.

She's been doing that more often, waving to him and saying goodbye. I imagine it's only a matter of time until she starts to hug him. She's changing around him, and changing at school, too. She's coming out of her shell.

We won't have much time since the other parents will be arriving with their kids any minute, but I'll take whatever I can to have Mason stay here with me.

I point to the coffee cup in his hand. "Any chance you were amazing and brought me a coffee?"

He smiles and runs his tongue along his lower lip. *Dear Lord in heaven, that tongue on those lips is sinful.* Why can't our stupid three dates be over? *Why did I even recommend it?* When this trial period is over, I'm going to climb this man like a tree—if he will let me.

I never gave him a chance to answer my question last night, too afraid of him rejecting me right off the bat. I mean, I hope I'm reading the signs correctly. And if I am, they all point to me getting to lay my hands on this muscular god.

"What if I did?"

"I would say you're the most amazing man in the world because our coffee pot sucks, and Colleen's coffee is the best."

"Oh, well, in that case, it's for you." He beams at me as I take the cup from his outstretched hand.

"Thank the heavens. I would have been sad if it really wasn't for me and you were just teasing me with it."

"Hey, listen, my sister, Mallory, has her gallery event this weekend to showcase Kevin's work, and I wanted to know if you want to come with me?"

"Like, as your date?"

He scratches the back of his neck and looks to the ground before meeting my eyes again, offering me a coquettish grin. "We can make it date number three."

I smile up at him, seeing his eyes alight with excitement. "Sure, but can we meet there? I have an appointment in Waterford Isle, and I don't want you to be late in case I'm running behind."

"It's a date." He lowers his voice so only I can hear, "You never gave me a chance to answer you last night." My heart jerks and my stomach clenches as I wait on bated breath for him to continue. "I want you, Hannah. And I hope to God you want me, too, because this is about to be really awkward if we aren't on the same page."

I swear, time stops. Somewhere in the back of my mind, I recognize parents coming in with their kids, and I offer waves and smiles subconsciously. Mason is towering over me, and while he's not touching me, I *feel* him. It's as if his soul is reaching out to mine, entwining us together in this moment.

He throws his thumb behind him where his truck is parked. "I gotta get to the site. I'll see you later, Hannah."

He looks around and when he sees nobody's watching, he places a chaste kiss on my lips. I gasp at the unexpectedness of it, and he smiles warmly. I press my index and middle finger to my lips, heat rising to my cheeks as he turns and walks through the front door. I can't help but stare at his taut ass and thick thighs in those permanently dirty-looking jeans of his.

What I wouldn't give to be able to sit in his lap...

Only when he drives away do I finally get my body to obey my command to turn from the door and get back to work. Taylor gives me a knowing smirk but doesn't say anything. Thank God for small miracles.

Mason: *Hey, so, I got a babysitter for Saturday night, and I hope this isn't too forward, but maybe you'd still invite me in for a drink?*

I can't stop the silly little happy dance that works its way out. Mason James, I would invite you in for a hell of a lot more than that. I stare at the words and blink a few times to make sure I'm not imagining it. Another one comes in after that.

Mason: *Unless you'd rather hit up Mabel's after, or Lucky 7. I don't want to be presumptuous.*

Me: *No, my place is good.*

Mason: *Great, then I'm yours for the night.*

I'm so nervous. I look down at the black, V-neck cocktail dress that shows off just enough cleavage to be classy, not trashy, and ruby red high heels I'm wearing. I picked this outfit out the same night Mason asked me to come with him to the event, but

I've second-guessed my choice only about a hundred times since then. Finally, I had to put my foot down and just say enough, wear the damn outfit.

Mason had texted me on Friday, telling me his friend Cody agreed to watch the kids so he's mine for the night. *Those were his exact words. Yours for the night.* Of course, my mind started reeling with the possibilities of what we could do. All of them lead back to him coming to my place and the two of us falling into bed together.

Jesus. Am I rushing things? We haven't even kissed yet, and I'm talking about jumping into bed with him. Well, not a true kiss. The kiss he surprised me with at preschool doesn't count. I know he wants me. He's already told me as much, so really this should be an easy decision.

I've spent so much time with Mason the past few weeks, and even more time texting or talking to him. I know so much about him, but at the same time, he's so guarded. Most of our conversations revolve around his kids, his family, or work. I know his wife died and his mom ran off, but I want more than that. I want to know the stupid inconsequential things, too.

I glance at the wall, knowing I should leave now if I want to make it there on time. The butterflies in my belly return and become stronger the closer I get to the gallery. The parking lot is already filling with cars, and I hope I can find him in this crowd. Small towns, not much to do. It seems as if everyone is here tonight, which means, unless this gallery is more interesting than us, people will talk.

I get out of my car and stand by the door, looking around at the familiar faces. Even in my four-inch heels, I'm still too short to see over the tops of some people. I receive a few cursory glances and smiles, but most people continue to move past me. His warm hand wraps around my waist from behind and he leans down, his lips close to my ear.

"You look incredible, Hannah."

"Mason," I breathe his name. I turn around, his arms never leaving my waist, and look up into his dark eyes. He's in a pair of gray dress slacks and a black button-down shirt that's been rolled to his elbows. I swear, the sight in front of me brings a whimper to the forefront. A freaking whimper. There's something to be said about a man who knows how to showcase his forearms. Especially ones that are muscular and tanned from outdoor labor.

He looks like the most delicious meal and I've been starved for days. I can't seem to get my mouth to form any coherent words; my lips just keep opening and closing.

"You'll catch flies that way, pretty girl." He taps my chin and I close my mouth.

He extends his arm for me, and I willingly take it. That's when I notice it. His left ring finger is missing a ring. It's the first time I've seen him without out. This can't be the first night, can it? I think to our other dates, and I remember distinctly looking at his hand and seeing the gold band there. The fact he chose tonight to not wear it makes me so happy.

"We just need to make an appearance, and after that, we can leave if you want. No pressure. We can stay as long as you want to."

We step inside the buzzing space, and I catch sight of Mallory. She looks relieved as she spots us and takes a sip of her wine before waving at Mason. I see her other brothers, Matt and Max, walking around, and it appears Matt has found Olivia Lancaster. *Interesting...*

Hopefully, since he's the resident movie star, all the town will be buzzing about them, and Mason and I can be left alone.

I know the last thing he wants to do is draw attention to a budding relationship, and I feel the same.

We start wandering around, looking at the artwork. Kevin's work is good. Really good. I'm not an art connoisseur by any means, but the paintings and sculptures produce a feeling of... ecstasy. The explosion of colors that cover the canvas, the swirls, valleys, and ridges of the paint strokes, it's wild but tamed. Every piece hanging on the walls stirs a new emotion from me.

Some paintings, with their deep colors and heavy strokes, invoke a feeling of drowning or loneliness. These ones give me the impression he was dealing with some difficulties in his life and used art to work through the emotions.

I've never been one to know much about art. I mean, everyone knows and loves Van Gogh, right? But this... Kevin's work... is so different. I can see one of these paintings hanging on my wall and not feel tacky for it. Mason slides his hand into mine and gives me a gentle squeeze when I've stared at a painting for too long.

"Wow, your sister's husband is really good. This one is my favorite so far." The painting we're in front of has swirls of burgundy, red, and black with flecks of gold throughout. I look up at him and he's not looking at the painting. He's looking at me. His eyes are focused on my lips. I lick them as my breathing kicks up a notch.

We're in the middle of a damn public art gallery, and he makes me feel like we're the only two around. His pupils dilate as he takes a step closer to me and brushes some stray strands of hair from my forehead. We're standing so close to one another that when my breathing starts coming out labored with desire, my chest brushes against his.

"Hannah? Can I kiss you?" I glance around, looking to see

who's watching us. He places his finger on the side of my face, directing my eyes back to his. "Don't worry about them."

I swallow thickly, trying to get my voice to work. When no sound comes out, I simply nod.

He holds my chin between his large fingers and lowers his lips to mine. It's a gentle caress, and when I press up into him, he grunts in surprise. I immediately pull back, feeling like a fool to try and rush whatever is forming between us. I start to apologize when he wraps a large hand behind my head and pulls me flush against him for the most explosive kiss of my life.

He controls it, the entire experience, because it's not just a kiss. I feel him surrounding me, even though he's barely touching me. He coaxes my mouth open with his tongue, and I willingly allow it. Giving him whatever he wants, even in a room full of people. He explores, only for a moment, before pulling back from me, leaving me a panting, wet mess.

"Can we leave?"

He smirks. "Thought you'd never ask."

CHAPTER FIFTEEN
MASON

My brothers already pulled my chain tonight when I told them I was going to spend the night with Hannah. I haven't had sex since Ella, and of course, they were offering me the most unhelpful advice. *Jack off in her bathroom before having sex.* Yeah, thanks, asshole. I'm not doing that. I just hope that she can forgive me if I go a little... prematurely. I'll make it up to her ten-fold.

We pull into her driveway, and I'm out the door in a flash, walking to the other side to open her car door. She takes my proffered hand and leads me to her front door. Before she can even put the key in the hole, I have her back pressed against the solid wood and my lips have found hers again.

She tugs at my brown locks, pulling me closer, and the moment she tries to take over the kiss, I grasp her chin between my fingers, holding her still, allowing me time to explore her the way I want to. She whimpers against me as I part her lips with my tongue and pull her pelvis flush with mine. I'm hard as a fucking rock, and when she grinds herself against me, I know we'd better stop if we are going to make it inside.

"Hannah, the door," I pant.

Her eyes are glassy as she licks her lips and nods. I can't help myself. When she turns around, I take her hips in my hands and pull her back against me, my hardened cock pressing into her delicious ass. She needs to feel exactly what she does to me and how damn much I want her.

I lean over her, my lips close to her ear as she fumbles with the keys for the second time. "Hurry, little Hannah, I don't think your neighbors will appreciate a show." I slide my hands around her waist, and as soon as I start my descent, she pops the lock open and pushes the door in.

I let go of her to step over the threshold as she flips a light switch, illuminating the entryway and living room.

"Drink?" she asks breathlessly.

I want to roll my eyes at the absurdity of her question. I might as well be a caveman for the subtlety I'm showcasing. I assumed the texts back and forth earlier this week were pretty spot on and screamed I want to get in your pants, but I still need to make sure she's comfortable.

"Sure. Whatever you're having." I wander into the living room, taking a seat on her loveseat while she hurries to the kitchen to get drinks.

"All I have is beer. Is that fine?" she calls out.

"Sounds good."

She sits next to me, her leg brushing against my own, amping up the fire in my belly, and holds the beer out for me to take. I murmur, "Thanks," and take a big gulp of the cold drink, trying to keep the urge to pounce on her at bay. I watch from the corner of my eye as she fidgets in her seat. She keeps shifting around, unable to sit still.

"Ants in your pants?"

She stops, the bottle top pressed against her lips, and then smiles, lowering it again. "It's um," she huffs a laugh, "it's just been a long time, and I'm... nervous." She ducks her head, her cheeks flaming.

Shit. I feel like a damned fool. I guess I really did misinterpret the texts. She keeps her eyes trained on the floor, her cheeks still a beautiful shade of pink. Her breathing is labored, and I can see her nipples pebbled under her sexy little cocktail dress. *She's absolutely stunning.*

"Hannah, we don't have to do any—"

"No." She meets my stare. "No. I want this, Mason. I-I want you."

I put the bottle on the table and pull her into my lap with a gasp of surprise from her. I hold her hip and wrap my other large hand around the back of her head, bringing our lips close. She opens her mouth on instinct, and I dive in like a man starved of oxygen and she's my life force. Our breaths mingle as I hold her against me, torturing both of us by not closing the gap.

She whimpers and my resolve breaks. I press my lips against hers, my tongue darting out to taste her, explore her. She twists my hair between her fingers and starts rocking her sexy, petite body over me. I press my hips up, seeking her warmth, my cock screaming in agony to be set free.

With deft fingers, I find the zipper to her dress and undo it, freeing her from the constricting fabric. She pulls the thin straps from her shoulders, exposing her bare chest. I groan into the kiss as my hands roam up her body and land over her breasts, pinching her nipple between my thumb and forefinger and eliciting a shaky moan from her.

Without breaking us apart, I stand and help her wrap her legs around my waist. Her heels clatter to the floor. "Bedroom?" I swear, all the blood has settled in my groin, making it almost impossible to think straight.

"First door on the right." She points down the hall before her lips find my neck and she starts sucking and licking at my thumping pulse. *Jesus, if we don't slow down, I'm definitely going to make a damn fool of myself.* I push open the door, and when I try to flip on the lights, she puts her hand over mine. "Not yet."

My girl is shy. "Hannah, I want to see you. You're beautiful. Please, baby," I plead. I want everything she's willing to give me, but I also want the things she doesn't even know she wants to give me. I'm a jackass like that.

"I-um," she stumbles. I put her on her feet and dip my head, sucking a nipple into my mouth and releasing it with a pop as she shudders, her body breaking out in goosebumps. I drop to my knees in front of her, pulling her dress down her hips and legs, letting it fall to the floor at her feet in a pool of fabric. I don't even bother removing her panties as I push my nose across her most intimate parts, inhaling her scent.

"Oh, shit." She grabs my hair and pushes my face toward her, urging me to continue. *Hannah may be a little shy, but she's probably about as dirty as they come.* Looks like I have my work cut out for me.

I flick my tongue over her and she mewls, and then I start to eat her out over her panties. Teasing her, never giving her exactly what she needs. Her hips buck against my mouth and she groans in frustration. I can't help the smile that crosses my lips.

"Tell me what you want, baby," I demand. She's going to learn to say it; otherwise, she's going to be edging for a long time. I've got all night, and if she feels half as good as she tastes, I'm going to come in three-point-two seconds.

"Oh, God. Please, Mason," she begs. I push her soaked panties to the side and slide my finger up and down her slit, never touching the bundle of nerves. I probe at her tight little hole and my dick throbs in response, wanting to be where my fingers are. She has a death grip on my hair, trying to pull me closer and put me exactly where she needs me.

"Tell me," I demand again. I'll make it a little easier on her; I'm not a total bastard, after all. I look up at her. Her eyes are closed, and even though her room is cast in darkness, there is enough light from the hallway that I can see all her features, including the crimson that's staining her cheeks. "Tell me you want me to fuck you with my tongue and fingers. Say the words, Hannah."

"I," she inhales deeply as I continue my ministrations. "Please, fuck me with your tongue and fingers." The words fly out of her mouth, and she ends with a groan as I graciously give her exactly what she needs. She tastes so good and is so unbelievably wet it's a wonder no guy has kept her.

I toss one of her legs over my shoulder so I have more access to her and press my thick index finger into her. Her body grips me so tightly that when my cock gets there, I know I really am screwed. "Baby, you're so fucking tight. Ride my face, put me where you need me." I push another finger in as her hips press forward and she moves over me, her fears dissipating as the moments tick on.

"Such a good girl," I praise.

"Jesus, Mason," she groans. Her body starts to stiffen, and she's fluttering around my fingers, on the verge of her orgasm.

"Don't stop until you come on my face, Hannah."

She rocks her hips forward and back, forward and back, putting me where she needs me, taking control. I lap and suck at her, eating her like she's a damned brownie sundae. I push a third finger into her and rub them against that magical spot inside her. I know a moment before she lets go. Her moans are so loud it's a good thing she doesn't share a wall; otherwise, everyone would know she's about to soak my face.

Her hips move faster until finally, she lets go with a shudder. I hold her, lapping at her, prolonging her orgasm until she's all but limp in my arms and is trying to wiggle away from me. I sit back on my heels, still in all my clothes, and look up at her almost naked form. Her breasts aren't big, but they're enough for a handful, the nipples a nice rosy hue. Her stomach is flat, leading down to flared hips. My fingers trail over her skin, mapping each spot.

I stand, pressing my lips to hers, allowing her to taste herself. She wraps her arms around my neck and moans into my kiss as her fingers find the buckle on my belt.

"Your turn," she says as she finishes undoing my pants and starts pushing them down my legs. When she starts to lower herself to the floor, I stop her.

She looks up at me, her big blue eyes half-mast, but questioning why I'm stopping her.

"If you suck my cock, I'm going to come in two seconds. I want to be buried inside you for the first time."

I drop my head back and groan as she rubs me over my boxers. I'm not a religious man, especially after Ella, but the amount of times Jesus's name has crossed my mind when it comes to her is absurd.

I pull off my clothes as fast as I can but keep my boxers pulled up and stumble around as my ankle gets caught in my pant leg. I almost go down, but I manage to save myself by leaning into her dresser. She chuckles, covering her mouth so I can't see her.

"It's not funny," I tease, even though it is. It's just like me to botch my first time out of the gate. I've been thinking of her for weeks now, wondering what it would be like to kiss, touch, and taste her.

I reach down and pull a condom out of my pocket, and she raises her eyebrow. "My idiot brother is smart sometimes. I swiped one from him, just in case. I don't want you to think I always have them on me." Matthew is so damned afraid of knocking a girl up that he double wraps it, even if she's on the pill. Don't ask me how I know this... I'd rather forget the conversation that led up to it.

She smiles. "I didn't think you always carried one with you, but I also wasn't sure, so I bought some, too." She indicates the box on the nightstand. It's a good thing she had that foresight because I'm sure once won't be enough tonight. I want her to remember all the places I was when I have to go home tomorrow.

I stalk toward the bed, and when she tries to move back, I grip her ankles and pull her down so her ass is at the edge of the mattress and her legs are on either side of my hips. My dick is painful now, and while he's happy to not be suffocating in my pants, he's still trapped behind fabric. She curls her fingers into the waistband of my boxers and pulls them down, my dick bouncing up, standing at attention straight at her. Her eyes are fixated on him. As she licks her lips in anticipation, he jumps and bobs. I tug at the small strip of fabric still covering her and pull them down her legs, tossing them on top of my pants. *Those are mine now.*

I roll the condom down over me and urge her to lay down, pressing my hand against her chest. Her heartbeat is fluttering out of control, much like my own. She's nervous for this... or excited. It could go either way. I lift her legs and wrap them around my waist as I line myself up.

I swear, everything happens in slow motion. I press into her slowly, her heat like a scarf wrapping around me. She's so tight, and it feels amazing. She moans and adjusts her hips, allowing me to press in a little further.

"Jesus, Hannah, you're so fucking tight." I'm trying really hard not to be the asshole and push into her hard and fast like my body is screaming at me to do. She deserves for this to be good.

"You're too big, Mason," she gasps. I immediately stop; I don't want her in any pain. She takes a few deep breaths, her legs relaxing around me, and she nods. "Okay, keep going."

Inch by agonizing inch, I slide into her until I finally bottom out. I can already feel myself building up, and I know I'm not going to last. It doesn't matter how many times I've jacked off since I met her, being in her is entirely different.

"Hannah," I breathe through my nose, my nostrils flaring as I try to hold back. "I promise to make this up to you."

She nods and I thrust hard and fast into her, her tits bouncing with each push. The sound of her wetness wrapped around me echoes through the room as I punish her with my cock. She tightens around me as if she's going to come again, and I want her to come on me so damn bad.

I try to channel my thoughts as I rub her clit and pound into her harder, faster, our bodies and breathing in sync with one another.

"Mason," she moans as she tries to push my hand away.

"Not a chance. Come on me, Hannah. Come with me." I hold her hand down on the bed.

And then I feel it. The most amazing sensation out there. She flutters around me, moaning and whimpering as her body convulses in pleasure. *Yes!* I groan as my own orgasm works its way down my spine and my balls lift, emptying into her.

I have *never* experienced sex like that in my life.

CHAPTER SIXTEEN
HANNAH

I just had sex with Mason. *Jesus fucking Christ.* I just had sex with Mason. The phrase keeps replaying over and over in my head as I float back down to my body. We're still conjoined at the waist, but he feels too good there, and I don't want to break the spell we're under.

He releases my hand, and I place it over my racing heart. I've never had sex like that. It was so... so... *hot.* He's demanding but caring and already seems to know what I like. Hell, even I don't know what I like half the time. Sometimes, it's like a game of Red Rover; can I reach the finish line or am I going to be trapped in limbo?

He unwraps my legs from their death grip around his waist and slides out of me. My eyes roll in pleasure. I just came twice, and I swear I'm ready for more. And *holy shit* I rode his face, and he made me ask him to fuck me, along with the praise he offered. That was the hottest and hardest thing to do, but it turned me on ten-fold.

As he cleans up in the bathroom, I slide up the bed and

wrap a sheet around me, trying to feel less exposed. He comes back out, his eyes traveling the length of my body.

"You said you were going to make it up to me, but I orgasmed. So, I'm not sure what you're worried about." I chuckle. *Ah yes, the uncomfortable jokes are starting.* It's is my go-to when I feel uncomfortable, and right now, us being this naked, even with the lights off, feels really uncomfortable. Is this when I ask him if he's my boyfriend? Or are we fuck buddies? Ugh, I'm really not good at this.

He laughs and shakes his head. "Yeah, I surprised me, too." He pulls his boxers up and climbs into bed next to me. I'm extremely aware of my nakedness now and pull the sheet up a little higher.

He sees me and smirks. "I've already seen you completely naked. You rode my face, and now you're being shy?"

I blow him a raspberry. "This seems more intimate some-how." I huff out a breath. "Close your eyes for a second, so I can get something on?"

He pops his brow at me but closes his eyes anyway. I wave my hand in front of his face, and when he doesn't offer a response, I jump up and run around the bed. I almost make it past him when his arm darts out and he grasps me around my waist, pulling me to him. I gasp and giggle as I flail my legs when he lifts me off the ground.

"I like this shy side of you, Hannah, but I really like the dirty side," he says, nuzzling into the crook of my neck. "You're incredibly sexy. Don't feel like you have to hide from me."

"Um, thank you?" I squeak out.

He kisses my bare shoulder, working his way up my neck, drawing goosebumps from me again. "Wanna shower?" The lights will be on. He's going to see me naked, really see me. On the other hand, a shower sounds so nice. My body is sticky from the multiple orgasms he gave me. He taps my nose, pulling me out of my thoughts. "Come on, I'll wash your back."

He takes my hand, leading me to the bathroom. I stand back as far as I can so I can drink my fill of this man. He oozes sex and confidence, and his tight ass doesn't hurt either. *It's bad that I want to pull his boxers down and have my way with him, isn't it?* It's too soon. We just finished having sex. Don't most guys need time to get it up again? I loved his take-charge attitude. I've always been with men who weren't as confident as Mason is. I felt as if I always had to lead the way, but not tonight.

Mason made all the decisions and I was left to follow. And follow I did. Inside, I'm still doing a happy dance. My inner emotions are seriously throwing the party of the century with how gleeful I am. The only question that's left is are we official?

I assume we are dating now. He told me he wanted me, but you know what they say about assuming. He turns to me after the water is warm and offers his hand to help me under the spray. I'm on full display, but he's still respectful and keeps his eyes on mine, to my slight disappointment.

He pushes his boxers down and off and steps in behind me, closing the curtain. I turn, offering him my back, and tilt my head back, letting the warm water cascade over my face and body. Mason's hands find their way to my form. He dances his fingers over my skin until he finds my hardened nipples and spins me around. His mouth covers one of the dusty pink buds, and he flicks it with his tongue.

I reach my hand out, feeling his hardened cock, and he moans around my nipple then pops off it, closing his eyes as I continue to stroke him. Without having his eyes on me, I take a moment to drink him in. Fully drink him in. Jesus, Joseph, and Mary. He is *perfect*. He must have been sculpted by a serious artist. An artist who definitely knew the way to make a woman wet.

He is covered in muscles, but not like some gaudy bodybuilder. No, these muscles have been sculpted from hard, manual labor, not at some gym lifting weights. The corded muscles in his neck tighten as he clenches his jaw in pleasure. Each time he tightens his hands on my hips, his biceps dance and pull deliciously.

Then, there are his abs.

His perfect.

Freaking.

Abs.

Oh! And of course, at the base of his abs, there is the deep vee that leads to the most perfect cock I've ever put my hands on. He groans and I look up at him, watching his face pinch and twist in delight to my ministrations.

"If you don't stop, I'm going to come again." When I don't stop right away, he puts his hand over mine and pulls me off him. "Not that I wouldn't love to come right now, but I'd rather get you off and then come inside you." He nips my ear and my breath catches in my throat.

We finish showering and he helps me into a towel, wrapping his own around his waist, shielding my eyes from the perfect view. I get into my pajamas as he gets back into his boxers and we both climb into bed. I feel like we're rushing things, but at the same time, I feel like I've known Mason my entire life. As if our souls were meant to find one another.

"Mason?" I ask when he pulls me to his chest, my ear pressed against him. His heartbeat is rhythmic and soothing, lulling me to sleep.

"Yeah?"

"Three dates are over. Where do we stand?" His deep rumble of a laugh jostles me, and I squeeze him a little tighter.

"I thought that was obvious, or do you normally sleep with random men after three dates?" he teases as he strokes my damp hair before kissing the top of my head. "I want you, Hannah. There are times I think it's too soon, because of Ella, but when you know, you know."

"So, you're my boyfriend?"

"Seven nights a week."

I scrunch my face, suppressing my need to squeal in delight. "What about the days then?"

He pulls back to get a better look at me, and I crane my head up to look at him. "You've got jokes, funny girl."

I smile and lay my head back on his chest to listen to his heart. "What are you going to tell the kids?"

"That you're my girlfriend. And I'll make sure to tell my idiot brothers to not make a big deal about it." He rubs his hand up and down my back, drawing small designs with the pads of his fingers. "I won't be able to spend nights over, though. This is kind of a one-off deal." He takes a deep breath. "And we might have to sneak around my house."

Oh. I know he has the kids at home, but the way he tells me that makes me feel like a dirty little secret. I've never dated someone with kids. Is that normal? I really don't know what to say to that, so I opt for nothing.

"Hey," he says quietly, tilting my head up with his finger under my chin. "Don't worry, we'll figure it out. In the meantime, I will very much look forward to drop-off and pick-up at school."

The sun is shining through a crack in the curtains, and I throw my arm over my eyes, blocking the light. Mason is curled around me like a cat, and his morning wood is pressing into my lower back. His breathing is still deep and even. I don't want to wake him up yet. I don't imagine he gets to sleep in very often. If I can just shift a little, I can get out of his grasp and get up to pee. I attempt to move as slowly as possible, and just when I'm almost out of his hold, he pulls me back.

"Going somewhere?" he mumbles into the crook of my neck.

"Yes, I have to pee. Let me up." I squirm in his arms until he finally releases me. I dart to the bathroom and close the door behind me. I glance down between my legs and see a subtle beard burn on my upper thighs, and I smile as I think back to riding his face. His mouth definitely is full of sin and promises.

"Want to go for breakfast?" he calls out.

"Sure, I'm starved."

"Mind if we stop at my place and get the kids?"

I finish washing my hands and open the door, leaning against the frame. He smiles warmly at me and cocks his finger, telling me to come closer. A wicked gleam is in his eyes. I smile, biting my lower lip, and shake my head defiantly.

"Don't make me get out of this bed to grab you, baby." He cocks his eyebrow and licks his lips. The motion reminds me of a hungry wolf. And I guess that makes me the sacrificial lamb.

"Maybe I want to be chased." I shrug a shoulder, refusing to budge.

"Good thing I like the hunt."

CHAPTER SEVENTEEN
MASON

*M*orning sex is so much better than I remember it being. Maybe that's because we didn't have to make it quick because of the kids and I got to take my time with her. Two orgasms for her, one dynamic one for me. I hold her hand in my lap, my thumb caressing the back of it as she drives us to my place.

She pulls into the driveway and turns off the engine. I lean across the center armrest and pull her toward me, planting a heated kiss on her lips. I know we won't have long before someone either comes outside or calls my damn phone. I pull back long before I want to. She blinks her eyes open and smiles wide at me.

I glance out the window as Amber opens the front door. "Show time."

I push open the door and jog up the steps toward my daughter. She's wearing a purple shirt that says "Science, like magic, but real" and a pair of jeans. Ella was big into making sure Amber knows it's okay to like science and math and to use her brain.

She notices Hannah behind me and tilts her head to the side. "Daddy, what's Miss Hannah doing here?"

"Ah, Hannah here heard we were going to breakfast and wanted to come. Is it okay if she comes and eats with us?"

Amber nods and runs back into the house. We head inside so I can get the kids ready, and Max is sitting at the breakfast bar, drinking coffee. He glances in our direction, smirks, and goes back to looking at his tablet without another word. Thank God he knows to keep his mouth shut.

Teddy slides feet first on his belly down the stairs with a high-pitched giggle. My kids really are damn cute. I look over my shoulder and see Hannah smiling wide. She fits here, with us. Just seeing her in my house, it feels right. I hope she feels the same way. I'm falling hard and fast, and if she doesn't feel the same, I may drown in sorrow. I'm not sure I'll be able to pull out of it this time.

"Hey, buddy, get your shoes on. We're getting breakfast." I pick Teddy up off his feet, planting a kiss on his chubby cheeks. He squirms in my arms until I put him down, then he runs to the front door where his shoes are.

Amber grabs Hannah's hand, and I pick Teddy up to bring him to the truck. The two of us get the kids settled in the car, and then we are on our way. She's a natural with them. I suppose that's one reason she began working at a preschool. She likes kids. I take her hand in mine again, and as much as I want to kiss her fingers, I need to ease my dating Hannah on the kids. I don't want them to think their mom is being replaced easily.

I park in front of Mabel's and we all walk inside, grabbing a booth by the window so we can watch passersby.

"Did you and Daddy have a sleepover?" Amber asks.

I choke on my burning hot coffee and start coughing to

clear my lungs of the liquid. I glance at Hannah, whose face is five shades of red.

"Um..." she starts.

"I want to have a sleepover with my friend Lucas from school, but Uncle Matty says I can't. But he's not my Daddy." Amber looks at me. "You gots to have a sleepover, so can I have one, too?"

"Boys and girls can't have sleepovers, Amber. If you have a friend that's a girl that wanted to sleep over, we can look into that if her parents will let her," I offer, trying to appease the little girl.

"But you're a boy and Miss Hannah is a girl, and you did a sleepover wif her."

Ella, when the hell did our little girl become so astute? I swear, I can hear Ella's laughter as I try to sort through this one.

"I was a guest at Hannah's house last night because your Uncle Matt and Uncle Max needed the car to get home. Hannah was too tired to drive me back home, and I stayed over."

"Why didn't you just drive home wif Uncle Matty and Uncle Max?"

The waitress puts down our meals and I start cutting Amber's pancakes, effectively ending the conversation. She is too focused on her food to remember I didn't answer her.

"That was a close one," Hannah says, leaning into me.

I glance around the mostly full diner and notice a lot of heads turned in our direction. I bite back a snarl that's trying to break free. I wish these assholes would mind their own damn business. Who's fucking who has always been the highlight of these people's lives. If there wasn't gossip, I swear, their world would turn on its axis.

"Daddy?" Amber asks.

"Yeah?"

"Are you and Miss Hannah dating?"

I look to Hannah, who gives me an encouraging smile. I take her hand in mine under the table and pull our interlaced fingers up on the table between our plates for Amber and Teddy to see.

"Are you okay with that?" I ask. Teddy is too busy eating his M&M pancakes and looking around at the unfamiliar faces to care.

Amber's eyes light up and her face cracks into a smile. One that's so big, I haven't seen it since before her mom died. I know she's smiled around my siblings, and probably even Hannah at preschool, but not me. This look, this smile from my baby girl is one of the best sights I've ever seen.

We are going to be okay. This is the start of her liking me again, not pushing me away.

"Yes." She turns her attention to Hannah. "Are you going to be having sleepovers at our house? We can watch princess movies and play dress-up, just like I did wif Mommy." Amber bites her lip, her chin wobbling as her eyes glass over with unshed tears. "I still miss her," she whispers.

Hannah reaches over the table and places her hand on my little girl's. "Amber, it's okay to miss her and the fun you used to have with her. But, if it's okay with you, I would like to try and fill in on some of the fun things you used to do with her."

"L-like makeup and painting nails?" Amber asks through a broken sob.

Hannah smiles warmly at her. "Just like that. You let your Dad know and we will make it happen." Hannah slides out of the booth and reaches her hand out for Amber. "Come on.

How about you and I go to the bathroom and get cleaned up, okay?"

Amber hops off the bench, taking Hannah's hand, and the two of them disappear behind the closed door.

I look at Teddy, who has syrup all over his hands and shirt, but he has a big smile plastered on his face as he eats the sugary breakfast. "Is that yummy, bud?"

Teddy giggles. "Yeah. I wike pancakes," he announces proudly before stuffing another bite into his mouth.

I lean back, folding my arms over my chest. Mabel comes by to refill our coffee cups, and I swear she winks at me and smiles brightly. *This damn fucking town.* Amber and Hannah come back a minute later and Amber is all smiles once again. Hannah sits next to me, her hand resting on my upper thigh. I moan quietly and close my eyes.

Lucid memories of last night and this morning flit through my mind as Hannah draws lazy circles on my leg. This woman makes me feel like a teenager again. Hungry and ready for more. I glance around the place, and when I see no one is paying attention to us, I take her hand and place it over my hardened cock.

Her tiny gasp in surprise is all I needed to hear. Yup, I'm officially screwed. Hannah is my kryptonite, and I'll gladly take a hit.

I drive us back to my house and get the kids out of the car. Amber runs for the door as Matt opens it for her. "Guess what, Uncle Matty?"

"What?" He leans over, so he's closer in height to the three-year-old.

"Daddy and Miss Hannah are boyfriend and girlfriend," she states matter-of-factly.

"Great, now the whole damn town really is going to know," I mutter as I glance back at Matt and his smug ass smile.

"Wipe that smile off your face, asshole," I call out, hoping Amber and Teddy are already somewhere where they can't hear me.

"Fat's not nice words, Daddy." Amber rushes to the door and peers out at us.

"Of course, she would still be listening," I grumble, taking Hannah's hands in mine. "When can I see you again?"

She bites her lip, suppressing her smile. "You're seeing me right now."

"Still going with those damn jokes, huh, funny girl?" I rub the stubble along my jaw, finding a way to ask her to stay without sounding too damn desperate. I mean, I am. I'm desperate to spend more time with her, and inside her. I swear I'll never get enough of her. "Stay over tonight."

She titters. "Tomorrow's a school day."

I place my hand over my heart, feeling the steady thump of the organ I thought had stopped for good. "I promise I'll have you in bed nice and early, Miss Hannah." I lower my voice and lean in close. "Although, I can't promise how much sleep you'll get."

"Mason, I can't promise your household will be able to sleep if I stay over. Not sure if you remember last night? Or this morning? I'm not exactly quiet."

I wiggle my eyebrows. "I can fix that. Come on. I'll sneak you in after the kids go to bed," I joke, which, if the way she's looking at me is any indication, she doesn't take it that way.

"I'm not going to sneak around, not if you actually want this to be real. I get you have your kids to think about..."

I place my hands on her shoulders. "Bad joke. I was joking. Amber and Teddy love you. The only ones in that house you have to worry about are the built-in babysitters and trouble-makers: Max and Matt."

"Max is running for mayor; how much of a troublemaker can he really be?"

"Stick around and find out. Come by tonight for dinner and pack an overnight bag. I'm making pasta."

"I'll think about it. Thanks for breakfast, Romeo." She presses up on her tiptoes and gives me a kiss before turning away and walking to her car.

CHAPTER EIGHTEEN
HANNAH

I'll think about it? Thanks for breakfast, Romeo? Yeah, I definitely sounded like an idiot. Who even says crap like that? Ah, yes, the answer is Hannah Elizabeth Bailey. Mason makes me so tongue-tied sometimes I can't think straight. I pull away from the house, and when I look in my rearview mirror, I see he's still standing there.

My phone vibrates with a new message.

Taylor: *Heard you and Mason are dating now.*

Seriously? Already?

Me: *I see good news travels fast. Who did you hear it from?*

Taylor: *One of the ladies in the hair salon saw you two this morning at breakfast. Chatty Cathys, the lot of them.*

Me: *You don't seem to mind spreading the gossip, either.*

I pull into my driveway and kill the engine, leaning my head back against the headrest. My phone vibrates again, and I fully anticipate Taylor's witty remark, but what I see makes me turn ten shades of red.

Mason James sent me a dick pic.

Holy. Shit. It's... beautiful? Is it weird that's the first thing I think of when I see it? The next thought that comes to mind is all the ways he brought me pleasure with that dick of his, and I squirm in my seat. The car is off, so someone must have set it on fire or something because I start to glisten. Sweat trickles down the back of my neck, tickling my flushed skin.

Mason: *Come tonight and I promise to make it worth your while. :)*

I fan my face, thankful I'm facing away from the street so no one can see me. I look around, making sure no one is around, and pull my shirt over my head, sitting there in my favorite lacy white bra. I snap a picture, making sure to keep my face out of it, and hit send before I can chicken out.

I scramble to put my top back on and all but run into my house, safe behind a closed and locked door.

Mason: *I love your tits, baby. I want them in my mouth again. Let me make you say all the dirty things you want me to do to you. Then I'll gag you with your own panties so you don't wake everyone up when I give you what you've asked for.*

Jesus, this man. Holy crap. I can't even form a coherent response. My breathing is ragged as I read his text over and over. I've never had phone sex before, but this man knows how to do it. Even reading his words is turning me on.

Too much. Too fast. If we keep going at this pace, I'll be moved into his house in a week. Neither of us is ready for that. I think we need to make sure not to spend every day together. He needs some alone time with the kids, and I need some alone time with my friends. *Yes, keep telling yourself that, Hannah, and maybe you'll believe it.*

> **Me:** *You are dirty, Mason. I like it. ;) We need to make sure we spend some time apart. I don't want your kids to think I'm trying to steal their dad away from them. Let's limit the sleepovers to twice a week.*

I bite my nail, knowing sending that over text was a total and complete cop-out. Flopping down onto my bed, I cover my face in the crook of my arm and groan at my stupidity. I don't actually want to slow down, but I know he needs it, even when he suggests otherwise.

> **Mason:** *You're right, but also wrong. Three sleepovers. No negotiations.*

I smile, glad he didn't totally shoot down the idea.

> **Me:** *Fine. Three.*
> **Mason:** *Great. I expect your sexy ass here tonight for dinner, and then I'm going to strip you down and eat*

you for dessert. Wear the sexiest pair of panties you own. ;)

Oh, lordy, I'm in for a wild ride with this man. Sexy *daddy* in more ways than one, it seems. I've never been a girl with a daddy kink, never really been into the whole BDSM thing. I mean, I've read *Fifty Shades* and a few other similar books, but they never did it for me—the restraints, gags, and spanks. *Okay, well, maybe the spanks.* So, why do I suddenly want to do any filthy, naughty thing that this man wants to do?

It's exciting, dating a man like Mason. Looking at him, and knowing his history, one would think he's totally closed off. And he was, I just needed to pry open the lock. I'm enjoying this side of Mason. He's playful and really dirty. I have never been with a guy that can turn me on with words alone.

I pull up in front of Mason's house and get out of the car as Max and Matt are leaving through the front door.

"Hey, Hannah," Matt greets.

Holy crap. A Hollywood movie star is talking to me. When did my life become so exciting? "H-hi, Matt. Are you guys not staying for dinner?"

Max snickers. "Like that fucker would let us stay here with you coming over. He's worried we'll embarrass him."

I can't help the smile that takes over my face as I bite my thumb, picturing Mason with his flushed cheeks, trying to make his brothers stop talking. "Tell me something quick," I urge.

Max's face lights up and a devilish glint appears in his eyes. "He was worried he was going to be a two-pump chump the first night you hooked up. Contemplated jacking off in his truck beforehand."

I giggle and snort, unable to help myself. It must have been loud enough because, when I glance up, Mason's at the door leaning against the frame, watching the three of us. Matt turns to see what I'm looking at and mutters something about visiting Olivia and scurrying away. Max, on the other hand, salutes Mason and winks at me before finding his way to his car.

I hold out a plate with cookies on it as a peace offering. "I brought dessert," I say as I step up to him. He blocks me from stepping foot in the house and leans into my space. His signature scent of sandalwood and pear tickles my nose.

"I told you, you're dessert." He nips my ear before standing straight as Teddy comes screeching to the door and clings to Mason's leg.

"Daddy, up." The little boy raises his arms up, and Mason obliges him and scoops him up, resting Teddy's little bum on his forearm.

"Hi, Teddy,' I say and wave to him. Teddy buries his face in his dad's arm, stifling his smile. "I brought you cookies," I announce proudly.

The little boy squirms in his father's arms, reaching for the plate.

"Not until after dinner," Mason says, putting Teddy down on his feet. The little boy runs away, calling out for his sister. "Come in." He kisses me on the cheek and guides me into the house with his hand on my lower back. "Where's your bag?"

"Not here. Tonight's not a good night to stay over. I don't want Amber to talk at preschool and tell the other kids. There are still a lot of people in this town that would have a heart attack if they knew we were sleeping together without being married."

He makes a face but nods in agreement. He leads me to the kitchen and pours me a glass of wine, then picks up his bottle of beer and takes a sip. "Dinner will be ready in a few minutes."

"Miss Hannah!" Amber comes running into the kitchen with a big smile plastered on her face. "Are you eating dinner wif us?"

"With us," I correct her preschool language, "and yes, your Dad invited me over. Is that okay with you?"

She gives me a big nod and runs away again.

"Wash up for dinner," Mason calls out to the kids. When he hears the water turn on, he advances on me, caging me in against the counter with his large hands on either side of me. My heart is fluttering like crazy. He must be able to hear it. My breath comes out in shallow pants as memories flood back to me of yesterday and this morning.

His perfect, soft lips are inches from mine. We are so close we are sharing the same breath, wrapped up in our own little bubble. Nothing else matters right now but Mason James. I lick my lips and swallow hard, begging him with my eyes to close the distance and put me out of my damn misery.

A soft brush of his lips, a diminutive flick of his tongue, and he pulls back.

The Cheshire cat grin on his lips tells me everything I need to know. This man plays dirty. Well, two can play that game.

CHAPTER NINETEEN
MASON

Dinner was great. Hannah, as always, was amazing with Amber and Teddy. Watching her with them, it's like watching Ella. She's kind, caring, and patient with them... and me. I know the reason she didn't want to stay tonight has to do with me coming on strong. I've always been like that. I know what I want, and I will stop at nothing until it's mine.

And Hannah is mine, even if she doesn't know it yet. Jesus, this woman has flipped my life upside down. Never in a million years did I anticipate I would find someone who makes me feel whole again. Especially in Falls Village. She's my new forever, and I will work my ass off every day to prove it to her.

I'm jumbled up inside, my emotions all over the place, and she is the only thing that feels right. Moving back to Falls Village was out of necessity. I couldn't take care of my kids on my own; I needed family. Ella's parents asked me to stay, but I couldn't. I needed *my* family in order to heal.

I stare at the dark-haired beauty sitting opposite me at the table as she hands out the cookies she brought. Amber and

Teddy scarf theirs down in an instant and ask her for another. She glances up at me, asking for permission. "One more, then time to get ready for bed," I announce.

She hands the kids another cookie each from the plate, and I take the one she offers to me. Damn, her baking is good. It reminds me of all the treats Olivia, Matt's newest fling, bakes. Although I need to hand it to my little brother, he seems to be keeping this one around. Maybe his playboy ways are coming to an end. She seems like a nice girl; she could be good for him.

"These are really good, Hannah."

She blushes. "I'll let the baker know."

"I thought you said you baked dessert?" I ask, confused.

She shakes her head. "I said I brought dessert. I picked these up from *Spill the Tea*. Colleen sells them and they're my favorite."

The kids finish their second cookie and try to convince me to let them have another. Instead, I make them say goodnight to Hannah and take them upstairs to start the bedtime routine. Teddy is first. He was fighting staying awake at dinner anyway, so I knew he would go down fast.

Next, I go into Amber's room and see her sitting on her bed, a book picked out for me to read to her. I usually only get to put her to bed when Matt or Max isn't home, and since one of them is usually home, it's been a while since she's let me do this. She's growing up so damn fast.

"This book, Daddy." She holds the book with a bear on the cover. She moves over on her twin bed, allowing me a small amount of room for my large frame. I toss my arm behind her, and she snuggles into my side, allowing me to kiss the top of her head.

I read to her, doing my best to throw in some different voices for the characters as she relaxes into my embrace. She points out creatures in the pictures as I read through each page slowly. By the end of the book, she's almost completed asleep.

I extricate myself from under her little head and tuck her under the covers, placing a gentle kiss on the top of her head. Quietly, I walk to the door, shutting it almost all the way. I look in Teddy's room one more time, then head back downstairs to be with Hannah. She's sitting on the couch, a glass of wine in her hand as she smiles up at me.

"You're really good with them, Mason. I'm not sure why you doubt yourself."

"I'm better with them now. You've been helping me with that." I sit next to her, my leg and shoulder grazing hers.

She scrunches her face. "How? We've only been talking for a short while."

I rub my hand over the back of my neck and face her. "Yes, and before you came into my life, I was a miserable grump who couldn't hold a conversation with my kids. Amber wouldn't let me tuck her in unless I absolutely had to. Teddy... well, Teddy doesn't know any different, so he's never been a problem. Amber is going to give me hell when she's older. I'm going to have to chase the damn boys away."

She smiles warmly. "Yes, I'm sure you will, considering she has a boyfriend at school."

Boyfriend? What boyfriend? This is news to me. I never see her hanging out with a boy or playing with one. Every muscle in my body tenses as I see my little girl's life flash through my mind. In moments, she's grown up and as beautiful as her mother. I'm walking her down the aisle on her wedding day. I'm not ready for her to grow up yet. "What? What do you mean she has a boyfriend?"

She places her hand on my forearm, and I relax under her touch. "Relax, Mason. Lucas and Amber play together all the

time. He tries to kiss her, and she runs away. It's harmless."
She looks at the time on her phone. "I should get going. Thank
you for a great night."

The two of us stand, and before we make it to the front
door, I back her into the wall in the hallway, pinning my arms
on either side of her. "You sure I can't convince you to stay
tonight? I never did get the dessert I actually wanted."

She places her hands on my chest and bites her lip as she
flexes her fingers. I trail the back of my fingers down her cheek,
neck, then the side of her breast. Her breathing changes,
coming in shorter pants as my fingers continue their adventure
south. Hannah's putty in my hands.

"Remember how good my fingers felt in you?" I lean in
closer, my lips grazing the shell of her ear. "What about my
tongue, and my cock?"

She whimpers and her knees shake. Just a few more
perfectly timed strokes on her body and she's going to cave.
"Tell me you want me to shove my cock in you again."

"I," she swallows thickly, her breathing quickening. "I..."

The front door opens, and Matt walks in, a big grin on his
face. Hannah pushes me away, her face red as a tomato, but I
oblige and take a small step away from her to glare at my
brother instead.

"Oh shit, sorry," he says, looking between the two of us.
"I'll ah—"

"No, Matt, come on in. I was just leaving." She stands on
her tiptoes and kisses me. It's chaste, and when I try to deepen
it, she pulls back. "Good night, boys."

I haven't been sleeping well since the night I stayed with Hannah. It's like my body rejects the idea of lying in bed alone, which isn't good because it's been more than a week and she hasn't stayed over once. She's definitely going to get a spanking next time she's here for not holding up her end of the bargain.

We talk every day when I drop Amber off and pick her up. I've since taken over that again, specifically so I can see her; plus, Amber has been talking to me again. She did tell the class that Miss Hannah has come over for dinner, and Hannah was worried about that, but she hasn't gotten any complaints from parents, so she has since calmed down.

I don't think there is actually a rule about not dating a student's parent, but it is frowned upon. Don't want others to think my kid is getting special treatment and better grades because I'm fucking the director. Honestly, the whole thing is ridiculous, but I know Hannah is worried, so I make sure to bite my tongue.

I look at the clock on my nightstand. It's almost time to get up anyway, so I start my day a little earlier. I jump in the shower and turn the water as hot as I can stand. All this manual labor for the town renovation is great exercise, but it's doing a number on my muscles. I stand under the spray, letting the heat relax me.

My mind starts to wander to Hannah, and I get hard instantly. It's not really a surprise at this point. The woman has had my balls in her hands since the day I met her, even though she had no idea. I quickly finish myself off and get dressed.

Me: *You've been slacking on your sleepover duties. I think someone is owed a few spankings. Stay over tonight.*

Hannah: *Good morning to you, too, Mason. I trust you slept well?*
Me: *You know damned well I didn't. Not after Amber walked in on me last night when we were having phone sex.*

It's a good reminder to lock my door when Hannah sleeps over. I'm pretty sure I'm on Amber's shit list again after that. I yelled at her because she came in to check on me after I had jacked off all over my stomach while Hannah and I were having phone sex. I yelled at her to close the damn door. What does little Miss Smarty Pants tell me? It's a bad word and she's going to tell on me to Miss Hannah. It should be an interesting ride to preschool today.

Hannah: *Ah yes. If it makes you feel better, I couldn't stop laughing after we hung up.*

Ugh, this woman.

Me: *I'm begging you, Hannah. Please. My dick is going to fall off soon if I don't get to have you again. Plus, you can meet the new dog.*

Matt went to the pet rescue to get a cat for Olivia, the girl he wants to bang but she won't put out, and came home with a dog for Amber. No, I'm sorry, not Amber but him. He told me Amber's always wanted a dog, but it will be his when he moves out. That girl is going to throw a hissy fit if he tries to take the dog away.

On top of that, he purchased the old community theater

and a place for Olivia and wants me to renovate both of them. As if I wasn't busy enough already, and have even more offers banging down my door. Every business in town is crawling to get an update to stay current with the whole town changing.

The only reason I even agreed to take on both jobs is because I know Matt has a good heart, and he wants what's best for everyone. Plus, he promised he would move out after it's done. That means all I have to do is have Max get his own place, and then I'm golden. I'll get my house back, and I won't have to listen to those two bickering and making fun of me.

Hannah: *Okay.*

I fist-pump the air in time for Max to walk into the kitchen and make fun of me. Oh, what a start to another beautiful day.

CHAPTER TWENTY
HANNAH

*T*his has been the day from hell. Well, okay, not really. It's just been a really long day and I'm tired. The text from Mason has felt like lead in my pocket. It's not that I don't *want* to spend the night. I do. I *really* do. I'm worried about what Amber and Teddy will think. We are supposed to be taking things slow. Yet, here we are. Sleepovers? Lots of flirting and sex? That's not slow.

Matt picked up Amber today, and as I waved bye to them, Matt couldn't help but smirk and wink at me. *How embarrassing is that?* I haven't seen him since that night as Mason has started picking Amber up in the afternoons to steal a few minutes of time with me. We may or may not have made out in my office behind closed doors for a few minutes one time.

Just thinking about that day makes my panties wet in anticipation. And then thinking about how good Mason is in bed just starts me down a rabbit hole I can't be in, especially at work. I packed an overnight bag this morning before I left the house, and left my bedroom in shambles. I had to find the right pair of pajamas that were sexy, but not so over the top that if the kids saw them it would be inappropriate.

In order for me to find the perfect pair, I emptied out two drawers over my bed and rummaged through the pile. Then I had to take the fastest shower known to man and get dressed for the day. The gray dress I'm wearing today, paired with low kitten heels, was the first thing I saw in the closet and could get pulled on in a matter of seconds.

It's not what I would normally wear to work, as it's a bit restrictive when it comes to playing with the kids, but I made do. Taylor, of course, commented, and Mason's jaw dropped when he saw the form-fitted dress. He growled in my ear, and I've had to keep my legs crossed for the rest of the day, warning off my impending need.

I finish picking up in the last classroom and head to the front, going to my office for my belongings, when there is a quiet knock on the door. All the kids have been picked up, but it could be a parent returning for a forgotten item. I hurry to the front door and pull up short when I see Mason standing there holding a bouquet of colorful flowers in his dirty hands. He's still in his work clothes, having not gone home yet.

I rush to the door and unlock it. "Mason, what are you doing here? Matt got Amber an hour ago." I can't stop the grin that splits my face as he hands me the flowers.

"I've been thinking of you in that dress all damn day. I figured you'd have to pop home before coming over and could put those in water." He holds his hand out. "Come here."

I reach for him, and he pulls me flush with his body, mine molding to his like it was made to be there. I whimper as he runs his index finger along my jaw and over my lips, tracing their shape as if he's committing it to memory. "I've missed you, Hannah."

"You saw me this morning," I state breathlessly. His chuckle sends a thrill down my spine and I bury my face into his shirt, not caring that he smells of sweat and sun. It's Mason, and it's alluring. I can't get enough of him.

I'm just fooling myself if I think we can take this any slower. I want him so bad it hurts when he's not around. I never pictured myself falling for someone like him. Someone who already has kids, who is a few years older than I am. I always pictured my perfect man to never have been married, no past family to worry about.

Yet, when it comes to Mason, I'm ready to jump in feet first. I already think of his kids as my own. Amber tells me all about what's going on at home, and it's clear that the bridge is mended between father and daughter. She talks about Mason with such love in her voice. She's little enough that this rough patch they hit will be mostly forgotten by the time she's a teenager.

"That's not what I meant, and you know it, naughty girl." He nips my earlobe and my knees shake. They have officially turned to Jell-O. Thank God, Mason is helping me stay standing because, if not, I would be a pile of goo at his feet.

"I've missed you, too," I admit. No use lying to either of us. "I just want to be careful with Amber." *The moment to show my insecurities and hope he doesn't bash them to hell.* "I don't want her to get any ideas if that's not where you see this going."

His surprised look is everything I didn't know I needed. "Hannah, I'm not sure where your pretty little head is at, but I thought I've made it perfectly clear that you're the one I want. You've helped mend the cracks in my heart and my family. I've wanted you to stay over because I want the kids and my brothers to get to know you more. I want Amber and

Teddy to know just how special and important you are to me."

That speech, though brief, was one of the best damned things I have ever heard. I'm still tangled in his arms, but I launch myself at him, my fingers tangling in his hair. Unfortunately, as beautiful as the flowers are, they have been reduced to the ground by our feet and completely ignored in favor of Mason's tantalizing tongue and hands.

I love you, Mason. I know it's too early to utter those four words, but I do love him. I can't help the way I feel, but I need to know he's there with me. I'm not putting my heart on the line like that unless I know he won't break it.

He tugs my hair, reminding me I'm still attached to him, and I pull back, my eyes shining with desire. His dark brown eyes depict his own want. It would be so easy to pull him into a room, even my office, and have him fuck me then and there. There are no cameras in my office, and no one is here but us. *Would he, though?*

"Mason, I want you," I pant against his lips. He growls in response and pushes my body through the open door. "The flowers," I gasp as he locks the glass door behind him, trapping the two of us here.

"Leave 'em, I'll buy you new ones if you want them that bad. I need to feel you, Hannah."

I whimper. "My office."

He takes my hand, leading me toward my small, tidy space, and walks me back to the edge of the desk, placing his hands on either side of me, caging me in. I slide my butt up on the hardwood and press my legs open as wide as the dress will allow. He pushes the dress further up my hips until I'm no longer restrained and he can stand flush against me. His hardened cock is straining against his jeans, begging to be set free.

"I don't have a condom," he says, rubbing his hands up and down my legs, goosebumps forming in his wake.

"I'm on the pill. It's okay with me if you're okay with it." I fist his shirt in my hand, holding him close to me, hoping that request doesn't scare him off.

He nods and undoes his pants, his motions hurried and frenzied. I know what he's thinking; he doesn't want either of us to get caught with our pants down, his literally down. I'm already wet. I have been all day, so I'm ready for him when he pulls himself free and pulls my panties to the side. I lean back, offering him a better angle as he plunges in.

No preamble, no warning, just a hard, primal fuck. It's like he's a different man, one consumed with need. His groans and pants of pleasure edge me on. It's incredibly sexy. I reach my hand down to rub my clit, and he places his hand over mine, exploring my hard nub with me. I move my hand away and put it over his, guiding his movements.

My entire body is bouncing off his as he plunges in over and over again. The sounds of bodies slapping and heavy breathing fill the small space, and before I know it, my orgasm is right there.

"Mason," I gasp. I wrap my legs around him, feeling his cock throb inside me. He's not going to last much longer.

"Come, Hannah," he grunts, not slowing, not stopping, only building my pleasure higher and higher.

On a gasp, the tight coil inside me snaps and I shake, holding him tight against me, not allowing him to pull out. He pulls my head back and buries his face in the crook of my neck, emptying himself into me and grunting roughly.

The two of us stay tangled together as our breathing slows to normal. I pluck a few tissues from the box next to me and hand them to him to clean himself up, doing the same for me.

He chuckles and helps me right my dress. "That is not how I saw this going in my head."

I smile and try my best to fix my hair. "And how did you see it going?"

"I was going to hand you the flowers. You would be thrilled to see me and give me a nice kiss, and when I tried to go for more, you'd push me away, telling me to wait for tonight. Make me sweat it out a bit."

"Well, I guess, next time, that's what I'll do." I hop off the desk and gather the rest of my items.

"Oh no, you can't give me all that and then take it away. That's just cruel." He tucks some hair behind my ear.

When we get to the front door, the flowers are still there, but it seems the wind carried them a bit further into the parking lot. He gathers them up, picks out a few crushed ones, and tosses them on the ground before handing the bouquet back to me.

"I'll see you soon over at my place?"

"I have my bag in the car. I can go home and change if you want, but I'm comfortable wearing this if that's fine with you."

"Perfect. Come on, Max is making dinner tonight, and I told him to make extra because you were coming. And Olivia has been dropping cupcakes and cookies off all week, so we have tons of sweets in the house."

Olivia's been bringing sweets by? As if he can read my confusion, he says, "She's dating Matt, and I've agreed to do the build-out on her shop. She feels she needs the James boys to be her official taste testers now as she tries new recipes."

"That's sweet of you to do that."

"It's for my own gain, though. Matt promised when it's done, he'll move out. I love my brothers, but I'm ready to not have them living with me anymore. The three of us have always busted one another's balls, and being adults hasn't changed that." He shrugs. "Maybe it never will. Mallory tells us we need to grow up all the time."

I love when he opens up about his siblings and his family. It makes me feel included somehow, even though I have never been there for any of what he's talking about.

We each get into our cars, and I follow Mason to his house. When we walk through the front doors, it's loud, and the kids are running around screaming. Mason tenses, and I know he's going to yell out at them to turn the music down or stop making so much noise.

I place my hand on his forearm and shake my head. "Let them be. They're having fun, which means we can have a few more minutes alone before I'm going to be subjected to the Spanish Inquisition."

"You won't—"

"You don't think your brothers are going to ask questions, which will then set Amber off asking questions?" I interrupt him.

"You've got a good point." He takes my hand and leads me up the stairs, away from the noise, and cocoons us in his semi-quiet room. He tosses my bag on his bed as I take a look around. It still has feminine touches, so he must have packed up his old room and brought it here, not bothering to change anything.

I pick up the family photo sitting on his nightstand and run my finger down the front of it, over Ella. She was beautiful. I can see what drew Mason to her. Her exuberant smile draws the viewer to her. I imagine she was the girl everyone fawned over to get close to.

"She was beautiful, Mason. I can see where Amber gets her looks."

He takes the picture out of my hand, looks down at Ella, and then places it face down on the nightstand. "She does look just like her." He gives a deep, heavy sigh. "It's hard to look at her sometimes. I see my little girl, of course, but I see so much of her mom. And then, it doesn't help that she has the same attitude."

He shakes his head and gives me a sad smile. I know he doesn't want to talk about her; I just want him to know I'm happy to listen when he does.

"Come on, I'm starving. I can't wait to see what the mayor cooked for dinner."

CHAPTER TWENTY-ONE
MASON

I've got to hand it to Max; he made a pretty damn good meal, and he didn't gang up with Matt to embarrass me in front of Hannah. I'm pretty sure Matt is afraid I'll stop working on Olivia's build, so he doesn't want to do anything to piss me off.

For the record, not that I'd ever tell him this, but I like the girl. She's good for him. Since he became a Hollywood star, he's been getting his dick wet in a lot of loose women. These are the type of women that want to trap a man because they can. I never really paid much attention, but Ella did, always concerned for him.

Olivia is just... different. He's a different man when she's around. He's always been kind and caring, but she brings out the best in him. Just like Kevin did with Mallory. Now, if we could just get the world's most single bachelor to settle down, I could quit worrying about all my siblings and focus on Hannah and the kids.

She fits right in here. Hannah helped me cut Amber and Teddy's chicken nuggets and even got Teddy to take a few more bites of food. Usually, when I ask him to, it's like pulling teeth. For her, though, he did it without complaining.

"Okay, kiddos. Bedtime. Brush your teeth and I'll be up in a few to help you get into bed," I announce.

"Oh, Daddy, do we haf to?" Amber complains. "I want to stay up and watch fa movie wif you and Miss Hannah."

"Yes, you have to. It's a school night, which means you need sleep." Teddy rubs his eyes, and Matt helps him up the steps to get ready.

"No. Miss Hannah, please, can I stay up wif you and Daddy?"

She smiles and shakes her head, kneeling on the floor in front of the little girl. "Amber, you need all the sleep you can get, so your brain can remember everything you're learning. It's like a sponge; it soaks up everything, but if you don't get enough sleep, it can't remember the things you learn."

"It's a sponge?" Amber's face twists in confusion.

"Kind of. Here, let me show you."

Hannah directs her to the kitchen sink and lifts her, putting her on the counter. I stand in the entryway, watching the two of them in delight.

Hannah picks up a dry sponge and shows it to the little girl. "Pretend this sponge is your brain. When it's dry, it doesn't hold anything." She turns on the sink and sticks the sponge under the running water, soaking it through. "But, when you get your sleep, it's like a wet sponge, and all that you learn gets absorbed. See?" Hannah squeezes the sponge as the sink fills with water.

Amber giggles and looks over at me. "Can Miss Hannah read me a bedtime story?"

"Oh, I don't think..." she starts, looking at the little girl.

"Sure, baby. As long as she wants to. Why don't you ask

her instead?"

Amber turns to Hannah, her best puppy dog face already in place. I swear, that damn dog has taught her how to perfect her pout more than anything. She has started taking to whining like Sparkles McGlitter, or whatever crazy name she changes it to. It's a new name every day; I can't keep up.

"Miss Hannah, can you please read me a story?"

Hannah looks at me for reassurance, and I give her a subtle nod of encouragement. I think she feels like she would be stepping on my toes, but honestly, I love the fact that my kids are just as smitten with her as I am. I need them to like the woman I'm falling in love with.

"Sure, Amber. Go get ready, and I'll be up in a few." Hannah helps her down from the counter, and my daughter runs up the stairs, yelling for Uncle Matt and telling him she's a sponge.

I wrap my arms around her and she buries her face in my chest, inhaling deeply. "You sure you don't mind?" Her voice is muffled against my skin.

I push her hair back and place a kiss on the top of her head. "No. I'm glad you're willing to help. The kids love you." *And I love you, too.* "You're great with them."

She stares up into my eyes, and I see unadulterated joy reflected back at me. I lean down to kiss her, and just as I'm about to deepen it, Amber calls for us from the top of the stairs that she's ready.

I take her hand and lead her up the stairs to the kids' rooms. She stands in the doorway of Amber's room, waiting to be invited in as I tend to Teddy and make sure he goes down okay.

"Daddy, story," he says, getting comfortable with his pillow and five stuffed animals he's dragged into bed.

"A short one, it's past your bedtime." I sit on the floor next to his toddler bed and stretch my long legs in front of me, settling in for a quick book. *Chicka Chicka Boom Boom* is the book tonight, and he smiles at me as I sing along to the words. It's so short that after only a minute or so, I'm done. I turn to look at the chubby cherub.

"I love you, bud," I say and kiss the top of his head.

"Love you," he replies back. "Daddy?" I stop with my hand over the light switch. "Mommy come home?"

My heart drops into my stomach. I pull a deep breath in through my nose and push it out. I take my spot at his side on the floor again.

"Te—" I clear my throat and force the tears to stay put. "Teddy, Mommy isn't coming home. She's living with the angels now."

He scrunches his tiny nose and eyes, trying to understand what I've told him. This isn't the first time he's asked. It was worse right after she passed away because he would cry and call out for Ella. When I would show up, he would cry and fight even harder, begging for his mom. I cried with him those times.

Each day, he called out for her a little less, and as thankful for that as I was, it broke my heart even more. It's only a matter of time before he stops asking altogether. This is the first time in about three weeks, so it's happening a lot faster than I thought.

"She happy?" he asks, his voice sounding so small.

"Yeah, buddy. She's happy. She wanted to stay with us, but she couldn't."

"Why?" He cuddles a Mickey Mouse stuffed animal closer to his little chest.

Jesus, this is hard. "You know how much Mommy loved

you?" He nods. "Well, she still loves you very much, but she had to go on a special mission. There are other kids around the world who don't have a mommy to love them like you have. She's helping spread love to all those other kids."

"Okay."

"Okay." I lean over and kiss him again as he snuggles down to sleep. "Love you, bud." I turn off the light and close his door. I can hear Hannah and Amber talking across the hall, so I pause to listen in, not wanting to interrupt them.

"Miss Hannah, you and my daddy are boyfriend and girl-friend. You can do sleepovers. Why don't you?"

She chuckles. "Because I want to make sure you and Teddy are happy with me dating your dad. And I don't want you to think I'm trying to replace your mom."

"You can be my new mommy. I like you, and Daddy is happy when he can hold your hand and kiss you."

"I'm happy when we do that, too."

I stand under the doorframe and watch Hannah finish tucking the covers over Amber before I step in to give her a kiss goodnight. The dog is curled up on the end of her bed, already fast asleep. *When Matt leaves, Amber's going to throw a fit when the dog goes with him.* We might have to take a trip to the shelter to get her one.

"Night, baby girl," I say as I kiss her forehead and step back. Hannah leans in for a hug, and Amber kisses her cheek before turning over to face the wall.

We step out and close the door, and I pull Hannah to me for a tight hug. After the conversation with Teddy, I need her. Her strength seeps through her pores and my body soaks it up.

"I heard." Those are the only two words she says as she wraps her arms tighter around me. "I'm here, Mason."

"Thank you, Hannah."

CHAPTER TWENTY-TWO
HANNAH

It was a rough night for Mason. My heart broke when I heard him telling Teddy why his mom can't be with them. Amber must have heard them, too, because she started telling me she wanted me to be her new mommy... and the idea didn't scare me.

I love those kids so much already. And I love Mason, too. He's genuine. And from the men I've dated, that's saying a lot. He doesn't seem to fuss about a lot of things. He wants his family to be happy and works hard to achieve that.

I'm lying in his bed, stroking his hair as he's curled around my body, clinging to me as if I'm his lifeboat and he's adrift in the sea. His even breaths are the only sign that he is otherwise asleep. We've been like this for most of the night.

After putting the kids to bed, we went back to his room and he told me about the night she died. He told me about the following week where all he did was drink and walk around in a haze, how his actions could have ripped his family apart. He was depressed and had to pull his head out of his ass quickly for the sake of his kids.

All this information he dumped on me, completely drained him. It wasn't long until he was asleep in my arms, snoring softly. I didn't have the heart to move from under him, so here I am, hours later, still in the same spot. It's still early, and neither of us has to be up yet, but I really have to pee.

I slide his arm off me and gently try to untangle him from me. He stirs and pulls me close again.

"What time is it?" he mumbles into my skin.

"About four a.m. I really need to pee. Mase, let me up." I pat his arm and give it a little push. He doesn't fight me on it. I get up, do my thing, and I'm back in no time.

He's lying on his back with his hands propped under his head, giving me the perfect view of his naked torso. Even in the darkened room, I can make out the lines and ridges of his muscles. I lick my lips, wishing I had a cool glass of water to quench my sudden thirst. He smiles at me and my knees shake.

"You coming back to bed or just going to stand there?" he teases.

I jut my hip out. "I was thinking of standing here and admiring the view."

He smiles at me and my world tilts on his axis. I make Mason James happy. He makes me so damn happy, too. I want to be a part of everything in his life. Our situation works.

If we got married and had a child or two of our own, I would love that, but if not, that would be fine, too. Amber and Teddy are the embodiment of Mason. They are perfect. *Slow your roll, girl.* No way should I be thinking of marriage yet. He hasn't said I love you. I haven't said it. Yeah, the sex is great, but that doesn't change the fact that we aren't there yet.

"Get your ass back in this bed, Hannah, and I promise to tire you out."

A shiver runs down my spine and I clench my thighs together at the prospect. He tosses the blankets back, and even in the low light, I can see him grab his junk and squeeze. Ready and willing as always.

I put my knee on the end of the bed and slowly climb up on all fours, doing my damned best to be sexy in my tight camisole and shorts. I crawl slowly toward him, keeping my eyes locked on his, watching his reaction. The muscles in his jaw tick and he tightens his grasp on his cock. If it's anything like the need between my thighs, I know *exactly* how he's feeling.

I toss my leg over him, straddling his thighs as he grips my hips. Agonizingly slowly, he trails his finger up the side of my body, touching every curve until he grasps my hair and tugs my head back. A gasp of surprise leaves my lips the same time he finds my neck and the fluttering pulse barely contained beneath my skin.

I rock my hips, his hardness pressing against my bundle of nerves. I've never been one of those girls who could get off like this, but damn if he doesn't make me want to. It's like every synapse is firing and my body is humming in anticipation.

"Yes, Mason," I moan as I keep rocking my hips on him, my fingers digging into his back. He still has my hair in his hand and is moving my head how he needs to find the spots that make me melt into a giant puddle of goo. It's not fair that he knows my body so well, that he can generate these sensations without even trying.

"Mason, don't stop," I pant as I rock even faster against him.

He drops my hair and holds my hips, helping to control my erratic motions. He dips his head and sucks a nipple into his mouth, biting down on the sensitive bud. I'm so close, I'm panting so loud that I don't hear the quiet knock on the door.

"Daddy? I couldn't sweep."

Amber pushes the door open, and I scramble to get under the covers and hide. My orgasm went from almost there to dead in the water before I could even think. I drop my face in my hands and pray for God to kill me now.

"Amber," Mason all but growls.

The little girl stops and her chin wobbles. "I knocked like you told me to."

He runs his hands down his face in frustration. "I know, baby girl. I'm sorry, you did good. Why can't you sleep?"

"I had a bad dweem and got scared. Can you come check for monsters?"

"Yeah, baby, I'll be there in a minute."

"What were you and Miss Hannah doing? It sounded like you were out of bref. Were you doing exercises?"

Seriously, could this be any more embarrassing?

"Miss Hannah was helping me scratch my back and it felt good." Amber nods and walks out the door. He looks at me and says, "Don't you dare move. We are finishing what we started."

I wake a little more than an hour later; I don't even remember falling back asleep, and Mason is lying beside me, watching me.

I put my hand over my face, shielding him from my view. "Ugh, creeper. Do you always stare at people as they sleep?"

"No. Just you. You do this twitchy thing with your eye," he points to his eye and tries to mimic what he *thinks* he saw.

I pull my pillow out from under my head and hit him with

it. "I do not, creeper. I think you just like to stare at people and freak them out."

When I try to hit him with the pillow again, he pulls me on top of him, wrapping his arms around my waist. I put my forearms on his strong chest to look down at him. "I only watch beautiful women, and only when I can't get the thought of how lucky I am out of my head." I take a deep breath as he pushes my hair out of my face. "I hope this isn't too early, because I've been feeling it for a long damn time. I love you, Hannah."

Don't cry. Don't cry. Don't cry.

"I don't expect you to say it back, but—"

"I love you, Mason." I kiss him, our tongues mingling, exploring each other. We let our bodies tell one another what words wouldn't be able to. I must be in heaven because I feel light as a feather and happy as a clam.

"I've felt this way ever since our first dinner when I saw you with the kids and how you handled Amber's breakdown over Ella. I thought it was too soon and pushed the thoughts away."

I can't help the smile that's on my face. "I love you, Mason. I love you, your kids, your family. I feel like I belong with you all."

He smiles warmly at me and nods. "That's why I've been staring at you. I can't get over how lucky I am to have you, and I'm scared like hell of losing you."

I take his hand in mine, intertwining our fingers. "I'm here, Mason. I'm not going anywhere."

"You were asleep when I got back, and I didn't want to wake you, but I also couldn't fall back asleep. You're beautiful, Hannah."

I turn red from head to toe. My body heats and my core aches for him. "Mason? Do we have time for a quickie?"

CHAPTER TWENTY-THREE
MASON

*H*annah loves me back. Jesus, I've never been more relieved in my life. I haven't been able to concentrate since she told me, too focused on her. Even at work, when she's far away from me, I still can't get her image out of my mind.

"Yo, Mase, watch out," Pete calls out for me. I clear my vision and notice the pallets of wood directly in front of me. "Pay attention, asshole," he calls out and laughs at me.

"Yeah, yeah," I say and walk around the pallets.

Pete catches up to me and slaps me on the shoulder. "Aren't you always the one around here telling us to pay attention? What's up with you?"

I smirk and brush his hand away. "I told Hannah I love her and she said it back." I'm giddy saying the words, but I school my features. Last thing I need is Pete holding this over my head. I can picture it now... and it's not pleasant.

"Really?" he asks, surprised. I nod slowly and take a deep breath. "Man, that's great. Good for you."

"Yeah?" I ask, not believing he's going to let me off the hook this fast.

"Yeah," he laughs at the end. "Why wouldn't it be? You two looked cozy at the gallery event, and Raina has been telling me the town gossip. You two were a hot item before news got out about Matt and Olivia. According to Raina, you two are old news. Why don't you come by next weekend? I'm sure Amber and Teddy will love hanging out with Aubrey, and Raina has been dying to meet Hannah."

Amber has been asking to see Uncle Pete and Auntie Raina, and it's only a matter of time before Hannah meets my friends. "Sure, let me check with her and see if she's free."

"Good, text me and let me know. I'll get steaks."

"All right. I need to call Avery and talk to her about getting together for Olivia's build. Find out when she's around to design it."

Avery was friends with Ella and we have stayed in touch. She moved to Falls Village and has been helping with the renovations as my interior designer. It's been working out great for both of us.

I pull out my phone and text Hannah instead. Avery can wait a few minutes, and I know it's afternoon nap time at the preschool and she'll be able to text me back.

Me: *I can't stop thinking about you, beautiful.*
Hannah: *I can't stop thinking of you, either.*
Me: *Are you free next weekend? My buddy Pete invited us and the kids over for dinner.*
Hannah: *I would love to meet your friends. I'm free. What can I bring?*
Me: *Just that sexy ass of yours. I might have to steal*

you away, and we can hide in the bathroom like a
couple of horny teenagers.

The little black dots appear and disappear over and over, and I know she's writing and deleting her response, probably trying for some smart-ass remark.

Hannah: *You're a horndog. Nap time is over. Later. I love you.*

I stare at the three small words that end her text. Seeing them written out brings a whole new perspective to the fact that we said those words to one another. A grin takes over my face, and I'm sure I've seen a few of the men walk quickly in the other direction. I don't think they have ever seen me smile. I shrug it off and get back to work.

"Amber, come on. We need to get to Uncle Pete and Auntie Raina's. Don't you want to play with Aubrey?"

Hannah is helping Teddy put on his shoes and stands up when he runs off in search of a toy. She looks amazing in a royal blue dress and a pair of flats. I wrap my arm around her waist and pull her against my side.

She looks down at her outfit and frowns. "You sure I'm not overdressed? You're in jeans."

"I'm always in jeans. And no, you look amazing. If you want to change, though, run upstairs and do it."

"No. If you say it's okay to meet Pete and Raina, then that's good enough for me. I just hope they like me."

"Pete and I have been friends for years. Trust me, they're

going to love you." I look up the stairs. "Amber Juliette, if you're not downstairs by the time I count to five, you're going to be in big trouble. One."

"Daddy, I'm coming. I'm trying to get Sprinkles to wear a dress like Miss Hannah."

A dress? What the hell is that girl doing? "Amber, the dog isn't coming with us. He's staying here." Amber screeches and yells out what a bad dog he is as the little white English bulldog runs down the stairs with this supposed dress trailing behind him.

"Daddy, hold him and put the dress on," Amber demands as her tiny feet stomp down the stairs.

"No. Amber, the dog is staying here." I take out my phone and snap a picture of the dog before he disappears around the corner. "I took a picture so you can show Pete and Raina when we get there. I'm sure they want to hear all about Sprinkles. We need to go, though. Grab your shoes and I'll help you put them on."

She stomps over to the door, grabs her shoes, and throws them toward us. My blood boils and I take a few deep breaths to calm myself. *If she doesn't stop this shit, she's going to get a swift smack on the butt.*

"Amber, is it nice to throw things?" Hannah steps in, picking up the shoes and walking them over to the sulking little girl.

"But I want Sprinkles to come," she yells and crosses her arms.

"Amber, just like in school, we don't yell or throw things to get what we want. Now, your daddy already said no this time. I'm sure Raina and Pete will be very excited to hear about your new dog and would love to see a picture, but we can't take him." She kneels on the ground and calmly helps Amber into her shoes.

"But I want him to," she protests and wipes her soggy eyes.

"I know, but not this time. How about I take a picture of you holding the dog, too, and you can show them. Would that be okay?"

Amber's eyes light up. "Okay." She darts away, chasing after the puppy, and wrangles him in her little arms.

Hannah takes her phone out of her purse and snaps a picture as Amber smiles the biggest, cheesiest grin in the entire world. Not even two seconds after snapping the picture, the dog wiggles his way out of her arms and darts off.

"Let me see," Amber demands, and when Hannah cocks her eyebrow, my little girl adds a quiet, "please" to the end. Hannah turns the phone, and Amber grins seeing the picture, clearly satisfied with the end result.

I pick Teddy up and Amber takes Hannah's hand to walk to the truck. We each get them into their car seats and we're off in no time.

"You were great with her, a natural. No matter what I do, I seem to botch it."

I know I'm being hard on myself, but I could have sworn this was easier before. My kids didn't talk back to me, didn't throw temper tantrums. Okay, Teddy hasn't thrown any yet, but I know it's coming. I've lost my touch.

"You didn't botch it, Mason. You're learning." She pushes a deep breath through her nose. "When," she lowers her voice, "Ella was alive, was she the serious one?"

I stop and think about it. I never had to do the disciplining because I wasn't home often enough. Ella was with the kids all day, so I guess I was the fun dad. I never had to worry about them. She did that, and I would swoop in and play with them.

"Yeah, I guess she was. I was just around to play with them. If she said no, I would back her up, but that's as far as it went. I never had to."

"But you have to now, and you don't know how. Get on their level, Mason. Kneel in front of them, listen to them, and you're going to be fine."

She takes my hand in hers and pulls it to her lips for a quick kiss. She's right. I can't replace Ella with Hannah. I need to learn how to care for my kids, and if she's willing to stick around to help, even better.

CHAPTER TWENTY-FOUR
HANNAH

*P*ete Roman pops out the front door and waves at us
as Mason pulls into the driveway.

"Pete Roman? Aubrey is in Amber's class. I know him. I
didn't realize that's whose house we were coming to."

Aubrey darts past his legs, and I can hear him shout for her
to be careful as she bounds down to the truck. Mason throws
open the door and scoops her up in his arms before opening
the back door where the kids are still seated.

"Daddy, get me out," Amber complains. She glances in my
direction and quickly adds, "please".

Mason puts the girl down and unbuckles Amber as I work
on getting Teddy out of the car. The house we are standing in
front of is in Fallen Hill Estates, the gated community, and it is
a sight to behold. Calling it beautiful would be an understate-
ment. I can hear the waves crashing along the shore, and as I
stare at the house, I feel like I'm in the Hamptons.

How the hell did he afford a place like this? I thought only
the richest of the rich in this town could afford to live here.

The house is white and wood siding with a large wrap-around porch. There are large windows in the front with curtains pulled back, giving it a homey feel. There are a few wicker pieces of furniture outside, and at the end of the porch is a fireplace. If this is what the front looks like, I can only imagine the inside.

I'm sure it has at least five bedrooms and three bathrooms, with all sorts of additional space for entertaining. I've never been in this part of town, but I've heard the rumors, and whenever one goes up for sale, I always look at the listings. *Pipe dream, but we all have them.* How does a contractor afford this place? He must have had a big savings for the down payment.

Mason takes my hand and leads us to the front door where Pete is waiting for us.

"Hey, Hannah. Glad you could come. It's always nice getting to know someone outside of my daughter's school," Pete says in a way of greeting. He smiles brightly as he glances down at our conjoined hands.

"I see I've been a conversation topic. Thanks for having us. I've never met your wife, so I'm excited to." I stick my hand out and he shakes it.

"She's inside. Come on in." He stands aside and Mason pushes me ahead of him, keeping his hand on my lower back to guide me inside.

Yup, I was right about the entertaining. The kitchen is to the right of the entryway, and it is beautiful. I don't cook or bake anything fancy, but if I had this kitchen, I'd want to. A beautiful woman with red hair has her back to us as she chops some fruit.

"Raina, meet Hannah," Pete says from behind us.

The woman turns around, and my mouth drops open. "Y-you're Raina Montgomery," I blurt out.

"Montgomery-Roman," Pete mumbles behind us, clearly annoyed at me using her maiden name.

Holy. Shit. I'm standing in Raina Montgomery's kitchen, and she's cutting up fruit like it's the most natural thing in the world. Celebrities like her should have a personal chef, not be doing it herself.

She laughs and wipes her hands on the front of her apron. "You must be Hannah Bailey. Aubrey talks about you and Miss Taylor often. Sorry, I haven't been able to meet you before now." She walks over to us and sticks her hand out for me to shake.

I must be in an episode of the Twilight Zone or something. There is no way this is real. I am a *huge* fan of hers. I've seen every movie she's ever made, and there may have been a time or two that I stalked gossip news sites about her.

Then it clicks. Pete Roman. I remember reading something about him and her tying the knot a few years ago. Mason nudges my shoulder, pulling me out of my star-struck moment, and I finally stick my hand out.

"It's a pleasure to meet you, Ms. Montgomery."

"Montgomery-Roman," Pete mutters again.

"Oh, Pete, hush. Don't get mad because people still prefer to call me by my maiden name. I still come home to you every night," she beams at her husband.

"Damn straight you do."

"Now, none of this Ms. Montgomery crap; I'm Raina. Any girl who can tame Mason is a friend of mine." She links arms with me and pulls me away from the men. I willingly follow and only glance back in time to see Mason give me an encouraging smile. "I've heard a lot about you. Let's head out to the back deck and get to know one another. Drink?" We stop in front of a fully stocked bar.

"Whatever you're having." I'm surprised I even managed to come up with that sentence.

She pours rum in a glass and tops it off with ginger beer and a lime wedge. I'm not sure what exactly I'm drinking, but if it has rum in it, it can't be that bad. I take a sip and hum in appreciation. It's good.

"A Dark and Stormy, in case you were wondering."

I smile. "I was, actually. It's good, thank you."

"I first tried it in the Bahamas and I've been hooked ever since. Come on, let's sit outside and get to know one another, and let the boys handle the food. I'm the one who made Pete invite you guys over. I wanted to meet the girl that tamed Mason James."

I blush. "I don't think I would say I tamed him." I take a seat opposite her and hold my drink, needing something to keep myself busy.

"I've known that man for years, and there have only been three girls to tame that man's heart, including you."

Three girls? Ella and me... so, who's the third?

"Amber."

I blink in shock. "How do you manage to know what I'm thinking?" I ask, astonished at her perception.

"Actress. You learn to read people, and you're like an open book. So, tell me about you."

I take a sip of my drink and start talking. I'm not a shy girl, by any means, but sitting here talking to a celebrity, I feel I have the right to be a bit flustered. I mean, I talk with Matt, but he's different. He's so... normal. Plus, to be honest, I was never the biggest fan of his. I would deny it if anyone ever asked, but his movies are usually just... eh. *Male Delivery* notwithstanding.

"So, Raina, what brought you here to Falls Village of all places?"

"A friend lives here, and it's a coincidence that it's where Mason is from. But also, my brother Elliott owns *At The Tip*. So, I have family around, even if it is my dumb younger brother.

"Oh," I start excitedly, "Mason and I have had dinner there. It's really good."

She leans forward and whispers, "Don't tell him that. He'll get a bigger head than he already has."

"Who will get a bigger head?" Pete asks as the two men join us. Pete lifts Raina up and plops her back down on his lap, and Mason drapes his arm behind me and tucks me into his side. The kids are running around the yard laughing and screaming in excitement.

"Elliott," Raina replies.

"Yeah, the last thing that guy needs is more people stroking his ego. His wife strokes him enough as it is." Mason chortles and Raina smacks Pete in the chest. He lets out an oomph and rubs the spot his wife connected with. "I mean, dinner's ready. Let's eat."

The steaks, salad, and roasted potatoes are amazing. It looks like Elliot isn't the only one in that family to inherit cooking skills. The conversation is light and comfortable, and I feel completely at ease now, despite the fact I'm still in Raina Montgomery's home.

"That was great, Raina, thank you," Mason says, leaning back in his chair, stretching out.

"Hey, I cooked the steaks," Pete complains.

"Yeah, and she seasoned them. I know not to mess with her."

Raina smiles and gives Pete a kiss on the cheek. "You did wonderful, honey."

A glance at the kids tells me everything I need to know. It's time for bed. I don't want to step on Mason's toes, so I lean into him and quietly say, "We should probably get the kids home and in bed."

He looks at them and nods. We gather our stuff, each of us carrying a half-comatose child to the truck, and say our good-byes. Raina gave me her cell and told me if Mason is ever annoying me, to reach out and we can have a girl's day. I will be guarding my phone from now on, but just in case, I put her in there as Raina Roman.

"I really like your friends, Mase," I say as we drive back to his house. "They're really nice."

"Yeah, they really are." He smirks and takes my hand. "They loved you, you know?"

"Yeah?" I ask as I gnaw on my bottom lip.

"Yes." He reaches over and pulls my lip from between my teeth. "Come on, you've been driving me crazy in that dress all day, and I can't wait to get you out of it.

CHAPTER TWENTY-FIVE
MASON

"*P*lease, Max?"

I hate begging. I hate it even more when it's my brother. He's gloating, and I hate it. The sly smirk on his face lets me know exactly how much he's enjoying my panic. Hannah and I have a date tonight, and I was going to be nice and give the boys a break by hiring one of the teenagers down the road, but she bailed last minute. If the fake cough and pathetic-sounding sick voice are anything to go off of, I would say there's a party she didn't want to miss out on.

There's not a hell of a lot to do in this town. Although, with the addition of so many new businesses and tourists that are starting to make their way through town, there's more to do than when I was a teen. Back then, it was either a house party or a bonfire at the beach. Since the state of Maine has put a ban on all beach fires, I can only assume it's a party.

"No, I told you, I have plans. Ask Mallory. She hardly ever watches the kids."

I growl in frustration. "She doesn't watch them because

she took them for almost a whole month. I owe her a lot for stepping up like that."

He sneers. "And what are Matt and I, huh? Chopped liver? Jesus, we moved in with you to help you take care of the kids."

I toss my hands up as my voice gets louder. "You don't think I know that and appreciate it?"

"You sure have a funny way of showing it." He lowers his voice. "Look, I'm sorry, but I made plans tonight."

I rub my hands down the front of my face in frustration. He's right. I know he is. "Fine, I'll see if Mallory can take them tonight."

Max nods and heads out of the house to God only knows where. I know he won't get into too much trouble, being the mayor and all. The last thing he needs is a scandal.

I call Mallory.

"Hey, Mase, what's going on. Everything okay?"

I sigh and rub my forehead. "Not really, my sitter canceled last minute. I wondered if you were up for babysitting the kids tonight? I have a date with Hannah."

I can hear her smile through the phone. "Seems like things are getting pretty serious over there."

I hate talking to my sister sometimes. She's perceptive and loves to point things out to me that are completely obvious. And in return, being her oldest brother, I deny everything. "Not any more serious than the last time I saw you and you watched the kids."

"Yeah, Kevin and I can come by in about thirty minutes. I expect pizza and dessert."

"I'll leave you cash and you can order whatever you want. Just don't load the kids up on sugar and try to put them to bed.

They will be up all night. Thanks, Mal. We shouldn't be home too late."

"We?" she questions.

"Goodbye, Mal."

I hang up before she can get any more questions out. The fact of the matter is, things are getting more serious between us, and I want her to move in with me. Matt is going to be moving out soon anyway, and Max, I'm sure, would leave tomorrow if I told him he could. There isn't much holding them here besides the kids.

Each of them would be much happier not living with me and, as I've heard Matt complain before, my *stupid* rules. I don't want my kids seeing certain things, so sue me. Hannah steps out of the bathroom, freshly showered, and her long brown hair drips onto the towel wrapped around her perfect, petite body.

"Did Max agree, or are we doing a date night here with the kids?" she asks as she towel dries her hair with another one.

"Mallory and Kevin are coming over tonight." I reach out for her and pull her warm, wet body against mine. "Which means you and I are getting away without the kids."

"Oh, sounds amazing. Where are we going? How should I dress?"

I kiss her forehead. "Casual, but nice. We're going to dinner first at *At The Tip* and then it's a surprise."

"You and your surprises, Mister." She pats at my chest and steps back. "Well then, how about you give me twenty minutes to get ready, and I'll come downstairs."

"Or, we can take twenty minutes, get dirty, and shower again?" I offer as a rebuttal.

She smirks. "Out." She points to the door, and I close it behind me, offering her privacy.

Matt is sitting on the couch as Amber and Teddy play with the dog on the floor. He looks up at me as I walk into the room.

"Is everything set for tonight?"

"Yes, I double-checked. Your dessert is set, and she's happy to have a taste tester."

I nod and rub my hands together in excitement. "Kids." Teddy and Amber both ignore me. "Your Aunt Mallory and Kevin are coming to watch you tonight. Behave."

"Yay, Aunt Mal is coming," Amber says, picking up the poor dog and spinning him. I'm surprised the thing hasn't puked his guts out with the number of times she spins him in excitement. Instead, when she puts the puppy back on his four legs, he runs circles around her, yipping and wagging his tail.

I look at Matt and don't even have to say it. When he moves out soon, Amber is going to kill him for taking the dog away. Which means we are going to have to go and get another one. Maybe. Mallory arrives a few minutes later, and just like that, I'm forgotten about again.

The life of a dad, I suppose.

Hannah comes down the stairs in a maxi dress and a light sweater. Her hair is down and straight, and she has a smattering of makeup flawlessly applied to her face. She looks perfect. I pull her into my arms and kiss her on the lips, soft and gentle. "Ready?" I ask her so quiet only the two of us can hear.

"Mal, money's on the table. Amber, Teddy, you'd better behave. Aunt Mallory will tell me if you aren't."

Teddy is smart enough to look a little worried. Amber, on the other hand, rolls her eyes at me. I swear, she's three going on thirteen at times. I raise my eyebrows at her in challenge, and she runs over to give me and Hannah a hug.

"Bye, Daddy. Love you."

Teddy runs over, throwing himself into my legs and squeezing them tight. I pick him up and kiss him on the cheek. "Bye, buddy. Keep your sister in line, okay?"

"Okay," he says, giving me one more wet kiss on the cheek.

I take Hannah's hand in mine and pull her toward the door, excited for a date that doesn't include my lovely children.

CHAPTER TWENTY-SIX
HANNAH

*D*inner was amazing, even better than last time Mason brought us here. The only downfall was he refused dessert. *What kind of monster doesn't let a girl have some chocolate?* He promised I would get my dessert with a wiggle of his eyebrows. Honestly, sex sounds amazing, but my heart was set on chocolate.

Dinner might have also been so wonderful because we are a real couple this time, or it could be because it's a date, just the two of us. The last time we were here, I was trying to help Amber open up to Mason. Let me tell you, she has no problem trying to put him in his place now. I love his kids, but it's nice to have an evening away.

Raina and I have been talking on and off since we had dinner at her house, and she's shared a few less than stellar stories about Elliot Montgomery, her baby brother. So, when the tall redhead introduced himself to us tonight, I had to stifle a few chuckles. Some of the stories Raina shared definitely wouldn't be considered polite dinner conversation.

Also, I'm friends with Raina Montgomery. How insane is

that? I go from small-town preschool director who hadn't gotten laid in *months*, almost a year, to chatting up celebrities almost daily.

I've been spending almost every night at Mason's house, and at this point, I'm starting to wonder why I even bother paying rent at my place. We're a great team, Mason and me. We just... *click*. Weekends are my favorite, besides the obvious of not having to get up for work. Mason and I will get up and he makes breakfast as I make coffee. Sometimes, Max and Matt join us, but most of the time, it's just us and the kids.

We feel like a family, and Teddy has even started crawling into my lap when we have a movie playing or if he gets tired. I know I'm not their mother, but I would walk through hell for those two kids, that's how much I love them.

Mason parks the car along a strip of stores on Main Street. Every place is closed, except one. The abandoned space has some lights on inside. There's no business sign out front, and as we walk up to it, I notice it's still in construction.

"Mason?" I ask as I reach for his hand.

Matt opens the door and smiles warmly at his big brother and me. "Took you long enough. Although, I should be thanking you. It gave me time to make Olivia scream my name a few times."

"Matthew!" I hear Olivia chastise from inside. "Mason, Hannah, come on in."

Okay, now I'm officially confused. I look up at Mason, and his smile is so bright it takes over his entire face; he's glowing.

"My surprise is seeing a half-finished store?"

He kisses my lips and pulls me against his side before sitting me down at a small high top.

"I'm doing the build-out for Olivia, and tonight we are going to be taste testers for a few of the goodies she wants to sell in the store. I know how much you like her baking and thought this could be fun. She's been bringing sweets to the construction sites as of late as well."

"That's why he's getting fat," Matt chimes in, barely missing the swat to the back of the head from Mason.

"I'm not getting fat," he grumbles.

If that was not the cutest thing for a grown-ass man to say, I don't know what is.

"It's okay, babe, I like your dad bod." I poke his belly to drive my point home. "Besides, how else am I supposed to stay warm at night?"

"Jeez, a man can't catch a break. Maybe I should be on a diet."

"Don't you dare, Mason James." I stand on my tiptoes and kiss him square on the lips. "I love you just the way you are. You're perfect."

Olivia carries a tray with several plates on it. When Matt tries to swipe one, Olivia sticks her leg out and kicks him, stopping his attempt. When she sets the heavy tray down, she shoos him from the area. My eyes widen to the size of saucers. I'm already stuffed from the amazing dinner, and now I'm looking at having to pound back six different desserts. Mason is going to have to roll me out of here.

"You don't have to finish them all, just a bite or two and tell me what you think," Olivia says as if trying to make me feel better.

"It's a sin to throw away baked goods, especially ones that look as delicious as these."

Olivia smiles and drops her head, clearly having trouble accepting the compliment. She puts a plate in front of us and rattles off the new concoction filled with chocolate and cream.

Honestly, as soon as I saw the chocolate overload, I tuned her out.

My spoon slides through the chocolate and cream cake and I pop it in my mouth, closing my lips around the metal. The flavors explode on my tongue. The chocolate is so rich and decadent, I didn't even know it was possible. The cream, while sweet, cuts the sweetness of the chocolate to give it a nice balance. *Oh my God, I want more of this.* I go in for another bite, and then another, and before I know it, I've eaten the entire thing.

Mason laughs and offers up the rest of his plate to me. I flush and push it back to him with a shake of my head. If the rest of these desserts are as good as this one, I'm definitely going to be ten pounds heavier when I leave here.

Each dessert is just as good as the last, and it's so hard to choose a favorite. I give myself a mental pat on the back for not finishing every bite of each of the five different desserts.

"Olivia, everything's amazing. I think you should sell all of them."

She grins. "Thank you, Hannah. Based on how you ate the chocolate bomb cake, I think that might be my number one seller."

Olivia actually packs up a few to-go boxes for us and even slips me in another chocolate bomb cake. I am beyond excited, and I hope the kids or his brothers don't get to it first. On second thought, so they can't get to it, I better take it by my place. I really should spend a night there so the landlord doesn't think I've completely abandoned it.

"Mason, could we pop by my place? I want to drop off my dessert there so no one at your place steals it. And then I'm thinking I should spend a night or two there. Vacuum, run the dishwasher, stuff like that."

"Sure. How about while we're there, we take a few minutes to have some fun before we have to return to the kids?" He bites his lip and smiles as he glances in my direction.

"Only a few minutes? I'm surprised, Mason. Normally, you can last longer than that."

"There you go again with your jokes."

We pull down my street and there are police cruisers and a fire truck down at the end. My stomach drops as we drive a little closer and see them in front of my cottage. The smoke billows into the night sky as the red and orange flames light up the night.

"W-why haven't I been called?" I pull my phone from my purse and see I have several missed calls from Frank, my land-lord. Somehow, the ringer was all the way down, so I never heard it.

Mason pulls over and I push the door open and stumble out of the truck, running toward the burning cottage.

"Hannah," Mason calls from somewhere behind me, but I'm too focused on my goal. *Get to my house.*

Mason wraps his large arm around my waist, pulling me back to him as I buck and try to get out of his grasp. One of the police officers spots us as Mason wrangles me still and approaches.

"Are you Hannah Bailey?" he asks.

"What happened? How did this happen?" I ask, ignoring his questions.

"Yes, she's Hannah," Mason says.

"Once the fire department has the flames out, we can find out, but it seems to have started in the back. Some of the guys are expecting faulty wiring."

Faulty wiring. I had asked Frank to look at an outlet for me months ago, before Mason and I started dating, because I plugged something in and it started smoking. Frank told me he took a look and everything was great. It's a random outlet that I don't have to use very often, so I didn't think much of it.

I look around and see Frank standing on the other side of the street on his phone. He spots me and looks relieved.

He jogs over to us. "I've been calling you, Hannah. Jesus, I'm so sorry about this but glad you're okay. I've been worried since you weren't answering."

I just stand there, staring at him, and then at my house. I heard what he said. I understand what he said, But I can't get myself to respond back. I vaguely hear Mason saying something to Frank, but I can't take my eyes off the burning destruction that was once my home.

All my stuff. *Gone.* How long did it take for the fire to tear through my things? Minutes? An hour? What if I had been inside? Would I have gotten out in time? Would Mason have to live through yet another woman in his life dying? What about Amber and Teddy?

What if? What if? What if?

"Hannah," Mason says directly in my ear, startling me. He rubs his hands up and down my arms. "Did you hear me?"

"N-no," I respond, shaking my head. "Um, I'm sorry. What?" *Jesus, I can't even form a coherent sentence.*

"Hey, it's okay." He kisses the back of my head. "Let's go to my place. The cops have your number and will call you when there's an update."

He slides his hand into mine, but I'm rooted to the spot, still watching. He gives me a small tug, and with great difficulty, I get my feet to move.

The ride back to Mason's is silent. He tried to talk to me once, but I just stared out the window in a daze. How quickly my life has been turned upside down. It's not even my things—

well, it's some of my things, but those can be replaced with the help of insurance. I feel like a part of me is gone along with the house.

I'm homeless. God, what a funny phrase, homeless. Very few people in their lives will ever be able to say they are homeless. And while I know I can stay at Mason's house, I still don't have a place to call my own anymore.

This night, this perfect unforgettable night with Mason just turned into one of the worst of my life. I wish I could rewind it and stop it after dessert.

Now, the only thing I want to do is crawl into bed and sleep for ages.

CHAPTER TWENTY-SEVEN
MASON

*H*annah hasn't left the bedroom all day, and I'm starting to get worried. She's barely eaten anything, and she hasn't talked to me since last night. She's in shock and trying to process her emotions. I'm trying to give her all the time she needs, but I'm not a patient man. She can't shut me out like that. Maybe I haven't made it apparent enough, but we're in it together, for the long haul.

I know she's upset, and I don't blame her, but it's not as if she's destitute. She can move in here with me and the kids, and we can get her stuff replaced. She's a smart girl, and I'm sure she had renter's insurance to cover her losses. I already have furniture here, so it's a matter of replacing her actual things.

I was going to ask her to move in with me but had been too chicken shit to do it. Now, if I ask, she's going to think it's out of pity because her place is gone. I sit on the edge of the bed and she glances over at me, her blue eyes so sad it breaks my heart. Her eyes are red and her face is puffy from crying on and off throughout the day.

"What am I going to do, Mason?"

I lay down next to her, and she snuggles in close, resting her head on my chest. "You're going to move in with me and the kids, and it's all going to work out. We'll get a claim filed with your insurance to replace your ruined things, and then I'll take you shopping."

She scoffs and looks up at me. "I can't move in here. Your brothers are going to kill me. And the house really isn't big enough for all of us."

I run my fingers through her dark locks and she sighs in content. "Matt already has one foot out the door; he's leaving as soon as I'm done with Olivia's place. And Max would leave tomorrow if I asked him to. He's ready to move out. I'm holding him back, and I know I need to let him go."

"What about the kids?"

"They love you, and I know you love them, too. You're already here so much as it is, why not make it official?"

I smile as I picture what it would be like having her here all the time. Stroking her hair to wake her when the alarm goes off and she doesn't want to get up. Weekend soccer games followed by brunch. A big Sunday breakfast where we all help in the kitchen while listening to music and dancing. Dress up with Amber, hide and seek with Teddy. The list is endless and each one makes my heart skip a beat.

I want that.

No. I *need* that.

I need Hannah, just like I know she needs me. I can feel it every time we're together. We complete each other, a whole unit. I couldn't ask for a better woman to be by my side—my new forever. No one will ever replace Ella, but Hannah... Hannah is my other half in ways Ella never was.

"I can't put you out like that, Mason."

I pull back to look at her and she sits up. "Why not?"

She sighs in frustration, her fingers playing with the hem of my t-shirt she's wearing. "It's only been a few months."

I shake my head, trying to figure out where she's going. "Okay. And?"

She tosses her hands up and then drops them with a thud on the bed. "Ugh, I don't know. Isn't it too soon? Isn't there supposed to be a set amount of time before you move in with someone?"

I laugh. "Who the hell told you that?" It's our relationship. We make whatever rules we want. She could have moved in here after the first date and I would have loved it.

"My ex."

I roll my eyes. "Jesus, that man's an idiot. Lucky for me, I guess. He told you that because he didn't want to be with you. Probably had a side hustle or someone else and was using you as a safe chick."

She frowns and scrunches her eyebrows. "What's a safe chick? Like someone he knows won't leave him?"

"Someone who he can show off to his friends and family without them batting an eye at his choice." I take her hands in mine. She glances up at me from under her thick lashes, her bottom lip worried between her teeth. She needs the reassurance that I don't see her like that; it's written all over her beautiful face. "Hannah, you are so much more than that to me. I love you. You're smart, funny, beautiful, and are the perfect woman for me and the kids. We need you. And if you're being honest with yourself, you need us, too."

After a moment of searching my face, she nods. The moment she believes me, her entire body settles, and her shoulders slump. "I do. And that scares me. I never thought I would find a man who already has a family. I thought, when the time was right, that we would start one ourselves." She takes my hand in hers. "But you and the kids, it's like you were meant for me. Like somehow, someone knew I needed you all."

That speech was perfect. She summed up my feelings for her, too, in just a few sentences. Ever since the night at the bar, I've felt like something has been pushing us together. Call it fate, kismet, whatever you want. She was meant to step into my life, to help mend the broken pieces, and she has. The man I was when she met me was too broken to help anyone.

Hannah helped put the pieces together. She made me see that I can love again. While Ella will always be a part of me, a part of this family, there's room for Hannah and the love she has to give.

"Jesus, Hannah, does that mean you're going to move in here with us?"

"Yeah, Mason. I'll move in with you."

I pull her to me, crushing my mouth to hers, my kisses becoming desperate. I need to consume Hannah. *She's mine.* She opens so willingly for me, allowing me free rein to explore with both my hands and my mouth. I wrap my fingers through her hair and tug her head back, angling her so I have room to kiss, lick, and suck the delicate skin on her neck. She moans as I flick her racing pulse with the tip of my tongue, just to hear the sinful sound from her lips again.

I press her down onto the bed and hover over her, my arms on either side of her head, trapping her below me. I lift my t-shirt up and pull it over her head, but not off, using the pull of the fabric to keep her arms planted above her, and continue my exploration of her body. Every curve, every divot, every marking and freckle; I want to memorize them all.

She lifts her hips in invitation to remove her shorts and panties. Instead, I brush my fingers along the seam of her shorts and press it up into her, feeling her soak the material.

She gasps as I press on her clit and start rubbing her. She spreads her legs wide, giving me access to use her as I want.

"Please, Mase," she begs in her breathy tone.

I slip my hand down the top of her shorts and panties, feeling her warmth as I press one finger inside her. She gasps and I cover her mouth with mine, swallowing her moans of pleasure.

"Just how I like you, Hannah. Wet and ready for me."

She bucks against my hand as I push her shorts down, kicking mine off at the same time. I'm desperate to feel her around me, to show her how much I love her. I line myself up and slowly sink into her wet heat. We moan in unison as our bodies connect, and I hold still, looking down into the most beautiful blue eyes ever.

"I love you, Hannah Elizabeth Bailey."

"I love you, too, Mason Frederick James."

She puts her tiny hands on either side of my face and pulls me to her as she wraps her legs around my waist. She controls the kiss as I control the thrusts. We are consumed with one another, so when there is a knock on the bedroom door, neither of us hears it.

The handle jiggles, and we each still. Hannah's eyes widen in fear as she tries to push me off her to cover herself. I learned after the last time Amber walked in on us to lock the door at all times if Hannah is over, or if I'm on the phone with her.

"It's locked," I tell her. "What?" I call out to whoever is there.

"Daddy, why is your door always locked?" Amber calls out, trying the handle again.

"Amber, Daddy's a little busy at the moment. Can this wait?"

I slowly start thrusting inside Hannah again, keeping the

momentum going. She swats my shoulder, but I smile at her and thrust especially deep so she squeaks in response.

"I want to play make-up with Hannah. She said we could."

"I did say we could," she whispers to me.

"Amber, go play with Teddy. Hannah is getting ready. She'll be down in a few minutes."

We hear her tiny footsteps as she retreats down the stairs.

"You have two minutes to come before she comes back whining."

I lay into her, thrusting hard and fast as her fingers fly over her bundle of nerves. The headboard starts hitting the wall, but I don't care. I want to feel Hannah come on me, and nothing, at this point, will stop me from experiencing that high.

I feel her tense around me. Her legs clamp down on my waist and she muffles her moans in my shoulder before biting down. *Jesus, that's new.* She's never bitten me before and I can't hold back. My entire body shakes as I come deep inside her with a groan of pleasure.

"You're amazing, Hannah." I kiss her glistening forehead. "I love you so much."

CHAPTER TWENTY-EIGHT
HANNAH

*D*o you know what is the most miserable thing to do in the entire world?

Dealing with insurance.

I swear, they give these people the most ridiculous script to follow just to try and get you confused and thinking you don't need to file a claim. I have had to talk with three different people, all who were unhelpful, and finally, *finally* got to someone who seems to have a brain, only to lose the person by an accidental hang-up.

I've been at work but was trying to sort this on my lunch break. I haven't had a moment to call again. Mason offered to help, but after being stuck on hold for five minutes listening to the same crappy royalty-free jazz music, he hung up. His red face and the number of times he said, "Fucking music" was enough to not ask him again.

It's already been a week since the fire, but I had to wait for the fire department to get me the report so I could file the claim. In the grand scheme of things, I didn't lose that much because the house was already furnished, but I did lose a few irreplaceable items that I'm heartbroken over.

One of them was actually my grandmother's engagement ring. My mom gave it to me because she didn't want to lose it when she and my dad were moving into their condo. I had always pictured I would be proposed to with that ring; I even had it sized for my finger. I don't even know all the specs for it, so I'm not sure insurance will be able to replace it.

Other items include some old pictures and a few wine glasses from places I've traveled to. All of which I won't be able to replace. Well, I'm sure I could replace the wine glasses if I ever could get away from work. *Maybe Mason and I will be able to take a vacation together.*

I can't believe I'm living with Mason now. It still seems like it's too soon, but he was right. It doesn't matter what others do, only what's right for us. And living with Mason, Teddy, and Amber feels right. Matt is moving out in two weeks, and he is over the moon excited for it. It could also be something to do with the fact Olivia is pregnant.

Max is still looking for the perfect place, but I'm sure it's only a matter of time before we are helping him move out and into his own. *I really wish he would find someone.* It seems as if all the James siblings have found their happily ever after but Max. A moment of self-doubt creeps up, but I squash it before it can take over.

Mason loves me, and I love him. I know he's it for me. My forever.

I look at the clock, resigned to the knowledge that I will have to try insurance again on Monday because they are closing in ten minutes, and there's not a chance in hell anyone is going to pick up the phone. *I know I wouldn't.*

The last kid was picked up a few minutes ago, so I'm free

and the weekend is finally here. Mason told me to *come home* as soon as I can. I still can't get over the fact we live together and his home is my home. I lock the door to the preschool and get in my car, heading to his—no, *our* house.

I pull into the driveway and his truck isn't there. I look up and down the street, wondering if maybe he had to pop out for something quickly, but it's nowhere to be seen. I walk inside and see a beautiful bouquet of pink dahlias, my favorite, on the kitchen table. There is a small envelope next to the vase with my name scrawled on it in Mason's slanted script.

Something beautiful for the most beautiful woman in my life. Can't wait for our date tonight. Wear something sexy.

Sexy? Half the stuff I owned was destroyed in the fire, including my favorite pair of undies. I have a decent amount of clothes over here, but I never brought over anything that I would be afraid of the kids or his brothers seeing me in.

I wrack my brain as I think of what I could possibly put on when I walk into the bedroom and see a box with a bow on it. I smile, loving this charade Mason has put together for me. I'm on pins and needles waiting to find out where he's taking me, and all these gifts are adding to it.

I close the door and lock it. I didn't hear the kids, but better safe than sorry. I untie the bow and lift the top off of the box. I pull the white tissue paper to the side, revealing a white lacy bra and matching panties. Under both items is another note with Mason's writing.

I love you in white.

What I want to know is who the hell helped him pick these out? I can't picture Mason walking into a lingerie store to pick something out like this. I glance at the sizes and note they are right, not that I would expect any different. A lot of my clothes are here; he even gave me my own dresser to use.

I rip the tags off the new undergarments and change into them as I poke around at the few clothes I have. Most of the items here are jeans, t-shirts, or work items. I have ordered a few things online, but I want to go to the mall to try things on.

"Something sexy?" I ask no one in particular as I rummage through. I finally settle on a pair of jeans and a fitted top. Mason once told me I look sexy in jeans, so I figure I might as well test the theory. I pull on a pair of Converse and pull the door open.

Mason's large frame is there, and I jump back with a quick squeal and start laughing.

"Jesus, Mason, warn a girl."

"Sorry, baby. I wanted to see if you liked your present and if you dressed sexy for me." He rakes his eyes over my entire form and smiles seductively.

"I did." I pull my shirt up, showcasing the new bra before pulling it back down. "And I don't own anything sexy. All my sexy stuff was burned in the fire, remember?"

He tips his head from side to side like he's thinking. "I don't know. You look pretty sexy to me." He extends his hand, and I slide mine into his. "Come on, we gotta get going before it closes."

"Where are we going?" He leads me out of the house and helps me into the truck without answering my question. "Where are the kids?"

"With Mallory."

"Okay, and where are we going?"

He gets to the highway and turns toward Waterford Isle, the bigger town next to Falls Village. It's where most people do their shopping and activities like movies and such.

"To replace some of the things you lost." He glances at me with a big smile on his face.

"I had to wear sexy things to go shopping?"

"Yup. Because whenever you take off your clothes, I want you to be thinking of me. Plus, I got us a room for the night. I plan on peeling you out of that outfit when we finally don't have to worry about kids interrupting us."

He pulls into the mall, and I can't help but be excited. New clothes, no kids for the night, and my sexy man. It sounds like a dream come true.

Five stores, five hundred dollars, and twenty bags later, I tap out. Mason has been so patient and kind through all of this, but I know he's dying to leave. He's been such a trooper and even tried to buy my clothes. I swatted his hand away the second he reached for his wallet. He did manage to sneak at least one purchase in for me, and I pretended not to notice.

"Oh, I want to pop in here and get something for the kids." I pull him into a toy store much to his dismay.

"Hannah, they have enough toys. You don't need to get them anything."

I ignore him and search the back wall that's filled with board games. So many of these bring back memories. I remember playing a lot of these, although the boxes look more colorful than they did when I was little. I spot the one I've been searching for and pull the box from the shelf, holding it up for Mason to see.

"Do you have Pie Face at home?"

He looks at me, at the box with a couple of laughing kids on the box, and back at me again. "No."

I beam. "Great. The kids will love smashing whipped cream in our faces."

"Great," he says, dragging the word out sarcastically. "Come on. Let's get out of here. I can't wait for you to try on the other item I bought for you. Plus, I haven't been able to see you in that sexy underwear I bought you. I'm *dying* to see that."

CHAPTER TWENTY-NINE
MASON

I'll never admit it, but I actually had fun walking around the mall with Hannah. It was cute watching her shop, and she's very good at finding a deal. There were a few items she liked, but when she saw they weren't on sale, she put them back. I proceeded to look them up online and ordered them in her size.

I want her to have things she likes, even if they are a little more expensive. I wish I could get more of her things back, like her grandma's ring. The night of the fire, after I got her to start talking to me when her shock finally started wearing off, she told me about some of the irreplaceable items she lost. I scooped her up in my arms and wrapped myself around her, trying to suck the pain away.

I know I can't replace it, but I can at least try. When she wasn't paying attention, I swiped her phone to get her mother's phone number. It turns out the ring was insured, and there was even a picture with the paperwork. I asked her to send me a copy of it so I can bring the picture to a jeweler and have a similar ring made for when I decide to pop the question.

There's no doubt in my mind I'll do it, it's just a matter of when.

Apparently, Grandma was loaded because it was a platinum setting with two quarter-carat diamonds on the sides and a three-quarter-carat diamond in the middle. The band isn't just solid, either. It looked woven, delicate. Very unique, and I could picture Hannah wearing it.

I step into the jewelry shop and my palms start to sweat. *Jesus, it's not as if I'm going to buy the ring and ask her tomorrow. Calm your tits, Mason.* I start looking through the cases, admiring the shiny stones and glimmering metals.

"Hi, can I help you?" A woman in her late fifties or so comes into view.

"Yeah, um, my girlfriend lost this ring," I pull the folded-up paper from my pocket and hand it to her, "and I wanted to see if you make custom pieces and can make a replica for me?"

The woman takes a look at the picture and reads the specs on the sheet. "I'm sure we could do something to match it pretty closely."

She waves at me to follow her toward the back of the store and knocks on a door. An older gentleman answers and smiles warmly at her.

"Will, this man is inquiring about a custom-made piece." She hands over the sheet of paper, and he takes his glasses off the top of his head and puts them on to scan the page.

He whistles as he continues to read before finally looking back at me. "I'll take it from here, Betty. Thanks." He turns his attention to me. "Hi, I'm Wilfred Sanders, the owner. Come in."

I take the empty seat closest to the door as he walks around his desk and settles in.

"Tell me about the ring."

I scrunch my face, not expecting that to be his request. I fully anticipated for him to spew a ridiculous number at me and have me willingly accept it because I want to be able to give Hannah the ring she always dreamed of. I've seen the number on the appraisal. That ring was worth a pretty penny.

"Tell you about it?"

He shrugs and nods. "You want to make a replica of a stunning ring, and I don't like to rip off anyone's work. Tell me why I should make this."

I lean forward, resting my arms on my knees, and lock eyes with him. "Look, my girlfriend's house burned down, and this was her grandma's ring. It was lost in the fire. I wanted to get it back for her."

He sits back, watching, examining. I feel like I'm under arrest and in a damn police precinct. An annoyed growl starts in the middle of my chest, and I swallow it back down, trying my damndest to remain calm. I lean back and cross my legs in front of me and my arms over my chest.

"What else?"

"What else?" I ask in disbelief. "Listen, do you want the job or not, Will?" I'm sure I can find another jeweler who will make it without asking all these questions.

"Perhaps. But you're going to be paying an arm and a leg for it. Humor an old man like me. Tell me why this is so important to you."

I take a deep breath and sigh. It's not like he knows me or is going to tell Hannah. I look around the small, tidy office space and finally land on the slender man in front of me.

"My girlfriend—"

"What's her name?" he cuts me off.

Jesus, is this man going to let me tell the story or not? "Hannah. She lost it in the fire, like I said, but she told me she hoped to have it as an engagement ring when the time came. I want to be able to give her what she wants. It won't be the exact one, but it will look like it, and I think it will shock the hell out of her."

I actually go on to tell him about how we met and just how special Hannah is to me. I'm not a man of many words, but Will makes me tell him about it anyway. He listens patiently, and when I'm done telling him my tragic tale, he smiles.

"I'll make the ring. I'll only charge you for the materials, though."

"Oh, Will. I can't ask you to do that. You're running a business here."

"Yes, and I like you. You remind me of me when I was younger." He points at me and waves his finger up and down. "You have more muscles than me, but still the same. I went through something very similar to what you went through, and if it wasn't for Betty out there, I'm not sure I ever would have pulled through. Let an old man do something nice for someone." He stands to make a copy of the paper and hands me back the original. "I can have it ready in a few weeks, is that okay? Or do you need it sooner?"

Sooner? I do like the idea of asking Hannah to marry me sooner rather than later. Really tie her down. *Unlike last week when I tied her down to the bed and had my way with her.* I smile at the memory, and when he raises his brow at me, I clear my throat. "A few weeks is fine."

"Great. I will call you when it's ready. Do you happen to have a picture of her I can see? I like knowing who I'm making pieces for."

I pull out my phone and open it to the most recent one I have of her playing with the kids. Her sparkling smile shines through. I can see just how happy she is in this picture. I always thought it was a nice one, but seeing it now, after telling Will about her... wow. She's life.

"I'll have it ready in a week." I look up at him, and he's smiling ear to ear. "You want to lock that one down as soon as you can."

The ring is more beautiful than I could have hoped for. Will did not disappoint, and he even added a few touches I think will really wow Hannah. Throughout the week, he asked me questions about her. He told me he wanted to design the *perfect* ring and even upgraded the center diamond to a full carat after managing to find one cheaper than he thought. I found myself answering everything and even sending him pictures of the four of us playing *Pie Face. She was right that the kids would love that game.*

I'm sure Hannah is going to love it. She's in Massachusetts for a long weekend visiting friends, and while I wanted to go, I had too much work here. I promised her we'd go together soon. I know she wants me to meet her parents, and as much as I hate these kinds of meetings, I do want to meet the man and woman who raised such a beautiful woman.

I'm standing in Alexander Hardware and Building Supply, which is owned by my buddy Cody, waiting for an order as I twist the ring box in my fingers. I haven't let it out of my sight since I picked it up. And since Hannah will be back tonight, I need to make sure she doesn't find it.

"Holy shit, did you get your girl a ring?" Cody asks, nodding at the black velvet box in my hand.

I tuck it back into my pocket as I look through the ordered items he brought out to me. "It's nothing. Is this everything?"

"I've never messed up an order for you, Mase. I may charge you a little extra, though."

He has a devilish glint in his eyes as he flips me off and laughs. He's an asshole sometimes, but I'm not sure where I'd be without him. We had a lot of good times together growing up.

"Thanks, Cody. Listen, I gotta run. Give my best to your mom for me."

I pocket the ring and wave as I walk out the door with my supplies. I promised Amber and Teddy we could build a tree-house. Not sure what I was thinking when I agreed to that fiasco. *Oh, yes, I was in a post-orgasmic bliss from an amazing morning blowjob.* Amber has been droning on about it since I agreed. Hannah quietly chuckled to herself, which makes me wonder if I was set up from the get-go.

CHAPTER THIRTY
HANNAH

*I*t's moving day! And by that, I mean I will only be living with *one* James brother instead of three. Matt moved out a few weeks ago and is loving life with his pregnant girlfriend, Olivia. Amber was sad about Matt taking the dog, and even tried to smuggle him into her backpack for school so he could live there instead. Mason promised to take her to the shelter to check out other dogs and to visit Matt often to see him.

Max is moving into his own house today, and Mason has been gone all morning helping him get set up in his new place. I know Max is just as excited as I am. I now only have two sets of ears to be weary of instead of three when Mason drags moans from me. I've watched him pull earplugs from his ears on his way to the bathroom one morning. He looked directly at me, smirked, and gave me a salute with two fingers. Needless to say, I was mortified.

I stayed back with the kids, and this is the first time I've actually been alone with them. It's working out well so far, and as it turns out, Teddy and Amber love being in the kitchen, cooking. When Mason left, I asked them if they wanted to help me make cookies for him, and both of their little eyes lit up.

I pulled one of Mason's white t-shirts over each of their little frames since I didn't have an apron, and we went to town. Amber did a great job of getting *most* of the flour in the bowl, and Teddy only got a few eggshells in the batter. All in all, it wasn't too bad, and I've got to hand it to the three of us, we made a damn good cookie.

Since I knew they wouldn't be able to help too much with the baking, we made sugar cookies, and I'm letting them decorate with frosting and sprinkles. Needless to say, Mason's white shirts are now blue, pink, green, and yellow, and the floor is coated in sprinkles. But the smiles on their little faces as they pick up their creations to taste their baking skills are worth it.

"Okay, let's get you kids cleaned up before your dad gets home and sees the mess we made."

I help the kids wash their hands and faces at the sink, and then pull their smocks off and deposit the stained shirts in the hamper.

"Go and play while I clean up, and when he gets home, we can show him your cookies."

"Okay," Amber yells out as Teddy chases her out to their fort. The treehouse is their new hideaway. Mason managed to build it between two trees, but only a few feet from the ground so if something happens they won't be too high up. He had to include a makeshift ramp because poor Teddy cried when he couldn't climb the ladder and join Amber up there.

I've finished cleaning the countertops and have the vacuum going when I feel a set of strong arms wrap around my waist. I didn't even hear him come in. Of course, I smelled him the moment he was in the room, so I turn off the vacuum and snuggle back into his embrace.

"You feel sweaty," I state, spinning to face him.

"You smell sweet." He leans down and kisses me on the lips. "Where are the kids?"

"Out back. We made cookies and the kids decorated. The counter and floor took the brunt of their skills, but they had a blast. They are excited to show you." I beam at him and nuzzle into his broad chest. "How's Max's new place?"

"Nice. I think he's going to enjoy his bachelor lifestyle again, although he did tell me he's going to miss the kids. And also a jackass comment about peace and quiet again."

My face heats up as I groan and hide behind my fingers. How embarrassing. Mason laughs and peels my hands away from my face and tucks me under his chin, planting a kiss on the top of my head.

"I'm going to take a quick shower, and then you and the kids can show me these delicious-smelling cookies." He reaches over and snags one from the plate and stuffs it in his mouth in one bite. "Mmm, good job, babe."

"Amber's gonna be pissed, you ate her favorite one." The lie passes through my lips easily enough, but the sheer look of terror on his face is what makes me start laughing.

I know he's still afraid of Amber getting mad at him enough to shut him out again, but she is so far past that. She raves about her dad. I swear, I've even caught Mason blushing once or twice. It was the cutest damn thing.

"Not nice, Hannah. Keep that up and I'll edge you until you can't take anymore, and then I'll torture you a bit longer, just to drive my point home that it's not nice to tease."

I shiver at the thought. I know he would do it, too, and take great pleasure in his luscious form of sexual torture.

He runs upstairs, and I head outside to get the kids. When Teddy sees Mason, he runs right into his waiting arms, and Mason scoops the little boy up as Amber takes my hand, pulling me toward the others.

"Come on, Mommy," she says. I'm not even sure she realized she said it, and it sounded so natural coming out of her tiny mouth.

I lock eyes with Mason, and he smiles warmly at us, not even phased by hearing her say it. At one point, I'm sure he would have gotten upset, thinking Ella was being forgotten about, but I know that's not the case. Ella comes up in conversation a few times a week. Mason will share stories with the kids and show pictures. He reminds them of her, how special she was, and how much she loved them.

I feel, in a way, that has helped him heal, too. Those conversations don't bother me, I actually love hearing them. I know just how loved she was, and it shows me every day how deeply Mason feels for those he loves. I know he feels the same way about me. He tells me and shows me constantly. I never have to guess where I stand with him.

"Heard you guys made cookies today. Amber, I tried one of yours and it was so good."

She grins at him and giggles in delight.

"I use blue and green, Daddy," Teddy says from his arms.

"I know, bud. I want to try one of yours next. Can you pick one for me?"

Teddy nods and wiggles to get out of his hold and run inside the house. The kids go in first and I hold him back for a second.

"Are you sure you're okay with that, with her calling me Mommy?" I worry my lower lip between my teeth waiting for his answer.

"Hannah, I love the fact that she called you Mommy. The kids love you and I love you. I know Ella is their real mother, and the kids know that, but the fact she sees you that way warms my heart. You're the mother figure in her life she needs."

I grab the neck of his shirt and pull him down to seal my lips over his. Mason James is mine. He's my forever, and he's perfect. I hear Amber's giggle and pull away to look at her standing in the doorway watching us, and I swear I see heart eyes reflected back. She's so happy for us. It won't be much longer until us kissing grosses her out.

Mason takes my hand and we walk into the house. Together, the imperfect perfect family.

EPILOGUE
MASON- THREE MONTHS LATER

Today is it. Today's the day I ask Hannah to become Mrs. Hannah James. Over the past three months, we have traveled to Massachusetts to meet her family and friends several times. Everyone adores Hannah just as much as I do, and Hannah has told me several times that her friends keep asking if I have brothers. *None that are available.* Yes, even Max has started dating someone. I've seen him wandering around town with Teagan Malloy, his old friend, but he's not sharing much with me.

I took a trip to visit her parents a week ago, and I spun it to Hannah as a boys' getaway with Pete instead. Imagine Pete's surprise when Hannah showed up with the kids and he was all but locked in his room for the day. Raina smuggled food up to him when Hannah and the kids weren't paying attention, but he bitched about it for three days after.

Her mom and dad were so excited when I showed up at their doorstep, but I was a nervous wreck.

"It's about time," Sandra, Hannah's mother, said as she opened the door wide. She reached up and pulled me to her

petite frame for a hug. "I'm so happy for you both. You're good for her, Mason, and she's crazy about those kids of yours." Apparently, this isn't as much of a surprise as I thought.

She pulled back and waved me inside the house. "Jerry, Mason's here," she called out.

I rubbed my hands down the front of my pants, attempting to dry them off before I shook Jerry's hand. "Hi, Mr. Bailey. I hoped I could take you out for a drink and we could talk?"

He slowly nodded his head and looked me dead in the eyes, his face completely neutral. I gulped as he gathered his jacket and walked out of the house to my truck without another word.

"I'm sure you know why I'm here," I said as I turned on to the main road.

"I do. But I want my drink first, and then you can ask me."

That effectively ended any conversation until I pulled into the parking lot for The Red Tavern. Jerry walked inside with the man of infinite swagger and sat down at the bar, ordering a gin and tonic with a lime wedge. I ordered a beer, and when the bartender put the drinks in front of us, I started.

"Jerry, I love your daughter more than anything in the world and wanted to let you know I'm going to ask her to marry me."

"You mean you're not asking me?" He took a sip and nodded to himself.

I shook my head. "No. She's an adult and doesn't need your permission, but I'm asking for your blessing. She makes me so damn happy, and I know I do the same for her. She's amazing with my kids, and they already think of her like a mother."

"Mason, Hannah has been crazy about you since the moment she met you. She called Sandra to tell her about this amazing single father she met and how she was going to help him with his kids. I didn't like the idea of her dating a man with *two young kids, but her heart has always been big. I know you don't need my permission, but you have it anyway. Let me see the ring."*

I smiled and pulled the velvet box from my pocket. He took the delicate ring between his fingers and examined it. He coughed and cleared his throat. "Where the hell did you find this?" he asked in disbelief.

"The original was lost in the fire, but Sandra had insurance paperwork and there was a picture. I took that to a jeweler and asked them to recreate it. He changed a few details, but I think she's going to love it."

"That ring, the one that was lost, that was my mother's ring." He examined it a bit closer. "Thank you, Mason. I know she's going to love this."

Mallory and Kevin arrive to watch the kids for the night. I told Hannah we were going to go to dinner, but I'm planning on surprising her by taking her to our spot to watch the stars. It's cold outside now, so I brought plenty of warm blankets and homemade cocoa.

Of course, my siblings know I'm going to ask Hannah to marry me and have been doing a terrible job at keeping it a secret. I swear Matt has found a way to almost slip it to Hannah only about ten times. He's worse at keeping a secret than my own kids are.

"We shouldn't be too late," I tell Mallory as I pocket the ring for the final time. Hannah comes into the kitchen in high heels and my dick hardens in my slacks. "Wow. You look gorgeous, but aren't you going to be cold?"

She looks down at her red dress and heels. "We are only

going to be outside for a few minutes from the truck to the restaurant. I'm sure I'll manage."

My girl, so clueless. Thank God I had the foresight to pack some warmer clothes for her and already tossed the bag in the truck. I place my hand on the small of her back, something I've learned she absolutely adores, and help her into the truck.

"Why does it smell like chocolate in here?" she asks as she sniffs the air.

I try my best not to panic and say the first thing that comes to my mind. "I bought us dessert already."

Her eyes light up. "Oh? What is it? Let me see." She turns in her seat, trying to find the treat, and I take her hand in mine, turning her back to face me.

"Let me give you one surprise. I know you don't handle them well, but just give this one to me." I lean over the console and kiss her.

She smiles at me and nods. "Fine, I'll give you this one. But there better not be anymore."

My girl is in for a rude awakening then.

"Okay, we've had an amazing meal, and now I'm ready for dessert. Let's go home," she says, settling into her seat.

"Not yet, baby. Soon, I promise."

She gives me a side-eye, and I can see the gears working in that pretty head of hers. Hannah won't let anything go, so it's difficult to surprise her with anything. I reach in the back and toss the bag of clothes to her. She opens it and pulls out a pair of jeans, then rummages through the rest of the clothes in there.

"What are you up to, Mister?"

"Get changed into something warm and find out." I shrug and look back to the road, turning onto the highway.

I'm sure she's figured out where we are going by now as she changes into the clothes. She pulls the dress over her head, and I'm met with my favorite pair of bra and panties. It's the white ones, the first set I ever bought for her.

I smile and lick my lips before biting the lower one. I give her one quick glance before focusing on the road again. "Baby, you sure know how to turn Daddy on."

She started calling me Daddy one night during sex, and it was so damn hot I came a few seconds later. She then told me when we first got together, she and Taylor would talk and refer to me as *Daddy*. So, of course, I poked fun at it for a while, until I realized just how much it turned me on to hear it from her.

She pulls the sweatshirt on and the jeans up, covering her perfect body in time for me to pull down the quiet side road. She lights up and sits straighter, trying to look at the sky from the top of the windshield. She knows where we are, and her excitement is overwhelming. She's practically bouncing in her seat.

"Is that dessert cocoa by chance?" She takes off her seatbelt and all but climbs into the back seat to find the warm thermos.

"Damn it, woman. Let me surprise you, will you?"

She grins from ear to ear and shakes her head. "Not a chance in hell, Mase. You know surprises make me cry. I don't like feeling off-kilter."

I'm about to turn your world upside down, baby. I park and get out, grabbing the blankets and pillows as she pulls the tailgate down and climbs up. The two of us lay the blankets out and set the pillows up behind us to relax against.

I put my arm around her and pull her to my chest, letting

her snuggle down into my warmth. My muscles are tense with nervous energy, but I try hard to relax. The ring box in my right-side pocket feels like a lead weight. I'm hugely aware of it sitting there. After tonight, I won't have to worry about Hannah finding it because it will officially belong to her.

It's been months since we've been here, but I know it's going to be the perfect spot. Hannah's been asking to come out here again, but I knew I wanted it to be even more special so I kept putting it off.

"Thank you for bringing me back here. I love it. I feel so special when I'm here with you." She snuggles in closer and turns to face skyward. I know she's searching the night skies for shooting stars, and I pray to God one comes.

Finally, about an hour later, we have an empty thermos of cocoa and the first shooting star of the night. Hannah excitedly gasps and points at it. Luckily, this time, I see it, too. I hate the idea of wishing on a star to get something you want, but I'm willing to tonight. I know how I feel about Hannah, and I know how she feels about me, but a little more luck couldn't hurt.

"Close your eyes, Hannah," I whisper as I detangle myself from her. She does so willingly, her dark lashes fanning over her cheekbones. "Make a wish," I whisper again.

She smiles and nods once. I have a few seconds before she opens her eyes. I pull the ring from my pocket, get down on one knee, and throw a silent prayer to the heavens above that she accepts.

She flutters her eyes open, smiles at me, and then drops the smile. "Mason, what are you doing?"

"Hannah. We started this journey less than a year ago, but I know you're the woman for me. You're the one who helped me get my life on track again, and you love my kids like they are your own. I couldn't ask for a better woman in our lives."

I open the box and shine a flashlight on the ring so she can see it better. She gasps and covers her mouth with her hand.

"Mason, where did you...?"

"It's not your grandma's, but it is a replica, with a few elements that make it special, just like you. I know I'm not supposed to say my wish out loud, for fear it won't come true, but do you know what I wished for on that shooting star, baby?"

Unshed tears make her eyes shine so bright as she shakes her head. "I can take a guess, but the phrasing might be a little off."

I smile wide, my muscles finally loosening. "Ah, there's my funny girl." I take her hand in mine. "Hannah Elizabeth Bailey, I have been in love with you since the moment I laid eyes on you. Will you do me the honor of becoming Mrs. Hannah James?"

She throws her arms around me with a squeal of delight. "Yes, Mason. A thousand times yes."

She pulls back and holds her hand out so I can slide the ring on her finger. I sure as hell hope I got the size right. She didn't have any other rings I could borrow to bring to Will so he could size it for me, so I guessed.

She takes my phone from my hands and uses the flashlight to examine the ring closer. "It's beautiful. How did you make it?"

"Your mom had insurance paperwork for the ring, and there was a picture on it. I brought it to a local jeweler and he recreated it, with a few touches that make it unique for you."

She looks up at me and wraps her arms around my neck. "I

couldn't have picked a better ring, and I can't wait to be Mrs. Hannah James." She gasps. "Did you ask my parents?"

I chuckle, thinking about poor Pete. "Yeah, um, remember when I was on a trip with Pete?" She nods. "Well, I wasn't, and he was trapped in his room that day." I laugh as I picture Pete again. "Raina had to sneak him food while you weren't looking."

She laughs and covers her mouth. "Poor guy." Her smile fades. "We don't have to do a big wedding. I know you've already had one."

"Hannah, whatever you want is what I want. Let's start with a date, and then we can plan it from there."

She nods, her smile returning. "I've always wanted a New England Christmas wedding. What do you think?"

"I think Christmastime next year then."

EXTENDED EPILOGUE
HANNAH- CHRISTMASTIME, ONE YEAR LATER

I can't believe the day is finally here. It still seems like a dream, like I'm watching someone else's life instead of it being my own. In a few hours, I am going to become Mrs. Mason James. We haven't spent more than a few hours apart since I moved in over a year ago, so last night was strange. Mason had to spend the night at the bed and breakfast, and my phone was taken away from me.

Seriously, we're already living together and have sex *very* regularly, so it's not as if this is going to be our first time. His sister insisted, so I spent the night with the kids, and Matt picked up Teddy this morning to get ready with the rest of the boys.

"Hannah, can you look up?" Bethany, my makeup artist, taps my chin, making me focus on her again.

I look up and she applies the liner to my lower lids. I blink a few times when she's done and look around me at the other girls in my party getting ready. My mom is snapping a ton of pictures of everyone as each girl sits for hair and makeup, most of them with a mimosa in hand.

Mallory is holding Amber on her lap as Amber watches some kid thing on YouTube. She's already in her flower girl dress, and Laurie, one of the hairdressers already added some curl to her hair. Taylor is here, along with my best friend from back home, Penny, and my sister, Kelly.

Penny moved to the city after we graduated from college and has been working as a landscape designer for a small start-up company. She's one of the sweetest girls I know and has recently found herself a sailor. Well, kind of. She did one of those 'adopt a soldier' programs and has been going back and forth with this man for a few weeks now. She seems a lot happier but won't tell me much.

Kelly is older than me by three years and moved to North Carolina with her now-husband and hasn't looked back. Which is why she is miserable in the cold and snow right now. She loves me, I know she does, but I think she would have preferred this wedding to take place in the summertime.

Everything is shaping up to be the perfect day. There is a storm that is promising a dusting of snow, which would be beautiful for pictures. I glance at the clock on the wall; only another two hours to go. I didn't sleep a wink last night, and I thought this day would drag on, but it has gone by in a flash.

Bethany puts the finishing touches on my makeup and holds out a mirror for me to see myself. My hair is already curled in soft waves that hang around my shoulders. Add the beautiful makeup and I look like a freaking goddess. My girls help me attach the veil to the top of my head, and my mom and sister stand on either side of me smiling.

"You look beautiful, Hannah. Mason is a lucky man," my mom says as she squeezes my shoulders tight.

The doorbell rings and Mallory answers it, coming back moments later with who I assume is the limo driver in tow.

"We gotta get to the gallery. The boys are already there, so we are going to have to sneak you in," Mallory says.

"Does it really matter? It's not like he hasn't seen me before. It's just another day."

She actually gasps in surprise. "It's not just another day. If he sees you before the wedding, it's bad luck."

"I know, I know. I'm not in my dress, though, so it's not like he hasn't seen it all anyway."

She shakes her head no as all the girls seem to push me out of the house. The limo driver holds the door open for me, and the girls all but push me in. Amber comes in next and crawls into my lap.

"Wow, I've never been in a limo before. This is cool." Her eyes are alight with excitement as I squeeze her close. "You look pretty. I'm happy you're going to marry my daddy. He's happy with you."

"I'm happy with him, and I'm happy with you and your brother, Amber. Thank you for letting me marry your dad." I snuggle into her cheek and then blow a raspberry on her, making her squeal in delight.

The girls all talk amongst themselves as I stare out the window, zoning out. It's a small town and doesn't take us long to arrive at the gallery. Mallory's space gets used as function space a lot, as there isn't a good place anywhere else in town. So tonight, we are using her location to get married, and Elliot is catering the wedding for us.

Honestly, it's not a big ceremony, so the space is perfect for what we need. The wedding and the ceremony both are taking place in the gallery, with a wait staff setting up the tables after tearing down the altar. Just a Justice of the Peace to officiate, and then it's good food, drinking, and dancing.

I feel like I'm the president or something as my mom and

girls form a barricade around me and usher me inside through a back door to make sure that, if Mason is around, he can't see me. The problem is, he's so much taller than all of us, I'm sure he would be able to look down and see me anyway.

We make it to the back room without incident, and Mallory takes Amber to be with Mason, so Mom, Taylor, Penny, and Kelly can all help me into my dress. And what a dress it is! A strapless, sweetheart neckline, A-line ball gown with beading on the bodice and a jeweled belt. When I tried it on, I knew it was the one. I feel like a princess in it.

Mom turns me around to see myself in the full-length mirror and I gasp, covering my mouth with my fingers. Tears well up in my eyes, and I have to blink them away. *I look like a damn princess, too.*

"Don't you dare. Bethany will kill you if you mess up those lashes," Taylor chastises, handing me some tissues to blot with.

I have never been more excited and more nervous than I am at this moment. In about an hour, I'm going to be marrying the sexiest man I have ever laid eyes on. He is an amazing father and outstanding lover. Seriously, I have never met someone who brings out such a dirty side in me.

I kick all the girls out, so I can have a few minutes to myself and take a few deep breaths as I look at myself in the mirror. The door opens and Mason is standing there in his tux. And what a sight he is to behold. The gray suit jacket showcases his broad shoulders, down to a tapered waist and thick legs. I can't wait until we are married and can come back here for a quickie as everyone dances and drinks. Just the thought of that makes my insides turn to mush.

"Don't you know it's bad luck to see the bride before you're married?"

"Don't you know I'm not superstitious?" he retorts.

I cross my arms, pressing my breasts up, and I notice him glance down. When he looks into my eyes again, he raises a brow and smirks. He holds his hand out in front of him, and I glance at it, unsure of what he wants.

"Give me your panties."

"Wh—I'm not giving you my underwear, Mase."

"Yes, you are, because you love to feel naughty for me, and what better way than no panties in a room of your family and friends as we say I do?"

I blush so hard I can feel the heat coming off my skin.

"Mmm, I love when you blush red for me, baby. I want to make your ass cheeks the same color."

"Mason Frederick!"

"Hannah Elizabeth. Don't make me climb under all that dress and take them off myself. You won't like how it ends." He gives me a devilish smirk. "Or maybe you would. I can tell you the wedding would probably start later, and your hair and makeup might need a touch-up."

It is like a sauna in here right now. I've been so stressed out about making sure all the details for the wedding were perfect, Mason and I haven't had much time for evening events. Sure, we have sex, but it's always quick. The dirty talk and foreplay went out the window weeks ago because I didn't have time.

"Don't you dare. Do you have any idea how long this took?"

"Tick tock, baby. Mallory is going to figure out I'm here in another minute or so, and she's going to rip me a new asshole. At least make it worth my while."

I bite my lower lip and huff before I pull the piles of tulle and fabric up to get to my panties. *I can't believe I'm going to get married with nothing on under this thing.* I slide the fabric off and hand them to him in a ball. He unwraps them and looks at the printing on the ass. *Property of Mason James.*

He grins from ear to ear before pocketing the panties. "Damn right you are, baby. You are getting more of these and wearing them all the time. Everyone will know you belong to me."

"Mason, I swear to God, if you are looking at her, I'm going to kill you," Mallory calls down the hallway.

"Gotta go. I love you, Hannah." He squeezes my upper arms and plants a kiss on my lips, leaving me stunned as he closes the door quickly behind him.

I hear Mallory yelling at him through the door and can't help but laugh.

Time to get married.

I'm hidden around the corner as Canon in D plays, and I'm waiting for my cue to walk down the aisle. My dad is next to me, and he keeps patting my arm like he's trying to keep me calm. Honestly, I think he's more nervous about giving me away than I am about getting married.

The part of the song comes, and we walk around the corner and into view of everyone. Everyone stands and I slowly start walking toward my future, my forever. Everyone else fades away, and the only person I can see is Mason. He's perfect. This is the moment I have dreamed about since I was a little girl. I didn't know what the man at the end of the aisle was going to look like, but I knew it would be perfect. And this moment is perfect.

Everything happens so quickly, and honestly, I can only half keep up. My eyes haven't left Mason's except to slide the ring on his finger. Since we didn't write our own vows, the ceremony was very fast and very simple. We can't be standing there for more than fifteen minutes when he pronounces us husband and wife and Mason plants a kiss on my lips.

He takes my hand and we walk back down the aisle until we are out of view of the guests, having a moment to ourselves as everyone starts cocktail hour.

"Hello, Mrs. Mason James." He wraps his arms around me, holding me tight to him. "It feels like it's taken way too long to be able to say those words. I love you so much, Hannah. You have made me the happiest man in the world today."

"I love you, too, Mason."

"Now, I believe it's time for a million pictures, and then some cake and dancing. But as soon as this night is over, I'm going to spend the rest of the time devouring you. I hope you weren't planning on sleeping tonight because I have a lot of plans in store for us."

"Promises, promises, husband," I tease.

"I like the sound of that, wife."

He wraps me in his arms and we look outside. Sure enough, a light snowfall has begun, and it is absolutely breath-taking. This small town that I knew nothing about has become my home, and I wouldn't want it any other way. I found my love and family here. The people may be a little cooky at times, but they are the best kind of people and I wouldn't have it any other way.

NOTE FROM ME

I hope you enjoyed reading Mason and Hannah's story as much as I enjoyed writing it. It was definitely a labor of love and I'm honored to be a part of it. Thank you to everyone who listed to me, and helped me through writing this book. You are right, it is definitely harder with a baby in the mix!

This collection has so many amazing stories in it, make sure to check them all out if you haven't already. You may just find a new favorite author or nine!

Falls Village Collection

ABOUT CARA WADE

Cara Wade is a daydreamer, and a lifelong teenybopper...boy bands forever! She would love to spend the day in the kitchen baking up sweet treats, but hates doing the dishes after. When she is not writing (or suffering writer's block) you can find her reading, hiking, or relaxing by the water. She lives in northern Massachusetts with her loving husband and the newest edition to her family, her baby boy.

ALSO BY CARA WADE

Sugar and Spice

Ever After

Grade A Girl: A MFM Novella

Hollywood Lust Series

The Publicist

The Playboy

The Starlet

Black Stallion Ranch Series

Infatuated

Enamored

Sin and Secrets Collection

RISE

High Rise Secrets

www.authorcarawade.com